SAND TRAP

SAND TRAP

DENNIS GIMMEL

Stellar Books

Published by:
Stellar Books
706 Impala Ave.
High Point, NC 27265

ISBN: 0-9712482-0-6
Library of Congress Control Number: 2002108279

Sand Trap.

First Edition
Manufactured in the United States of America
1 2 3 4 5 6 7 8 9 10

For Ginny & Arnold Gimmel, my mom & dad...thanks!

A special thanks to these friends who worked hard to make this a better book:

Stacy Johnson, Brenda Frazer, Cara Lenfesty, and, my wife, Rosemary.

CHAPTER 1

I T WAS A HOT EARLY FALL DAY. The Carolina low country's only relief was a gentle breeze that whipped through the pines and palmettos. Just twenty years before, this area was a swamp – a swamp waiting for the inevitable expansion of the Beach. Spurred on by greed and visions of opportunity, this swamp, like millions of other acres of swamp along the "Golden Strand," went the way of progress: golf courses, outlet malls, restaurants, time-shares, strip-malls, retirement communities, and pavement. The constant pat of lawn sprinklers and the occasional rattle of a cell-phone now replaced the age-old serenity of the quiet marsh.

In many ways they were just ordinary young people - ordinary young people caught up in the world they chose. Like several thousand people in the Myrtle Beach area, their livelihood revolved around a golf course. This group had more on their minds than grass seed and fertilizer, however. They were caught up in a different kind of game.

*   *   *   *

"What ya got, man? The suspense is killing us."

Ted Miller managed a slight grin and laid down a pair of twos.

Larry Holder shook his head and laughed, looking at Ted in amazement. "Eight bucks on a pair of twos... wow!" he exclaimed. Ted's playing partner, Marie, was fuming. "You better get your old man in here," Larry said to her with a big smile on his face. "Your partner is retarded."

"Damn it, Ted. Since when do we up the bet when we ain't holding nothing?" Marie said throwing her cards on the table. "I can't believe you!"

"Deal them up. I smell money," Larry added as he started to shuffle the deck.

"No way. This party's over," Marie said, getting up from the table. "This ain't funny, damn it," she said looking around.

"Touchy, touchy.... You have heard of bluffing?" Ted asked her.

"Get a brain!" Marie said staring back at him.

"Shhhhhhhhh...my mother's on the phone, ok?" Hannah Mason said over the roar. She walked toward the back of the work barn clutching her cell phone. Her husband, Mike, sat near the card game with his feet propped up listening to the radio. His hobby was short wave radio. He was tuned into late breaking cricket scores from Sydney.

The Saturday morning card game in the "Grounds Barn" at Droughbrigh Country Club was moving along, or not moving along as usual. They were always oscillating between laughing or bitching about something. An outsider might think they didn't get along. That would not be accurate. They were just a spirited bunch.

The barn crew always worked the first Saturday of every month. The Grounds Barn was their exclusive domain. The crew consisted of three couples: Larry and Bobbi Holder, Sam and Marie Conner, Mike and Hannah Mason, and a single guy by the name of Ted Miller.

Larry, Sam, Mike, and Ted all met ten years before while stationed at the naval base in Charleston, South Carolina. As luck would have it, a contact led to a drunken party, that led to an introduction, that led to their current job.

*   *   *   *

Nine years previous:

"What do you think?" Ted Miller asked. Ted was standing next to the equipment, leaning toward the face of the scope. It was all he could do to stay awake.

Larry Holder and Ted Miller were Third Class Electronic Technicians in the U. S. Navy. Their current duty station was a radar-training site at the Charleston Naval Shipyard. Their job was to keep the radar equipment operating. Radar-men from the Eastern Fleet came to Charleston for training on a variety of subjects.

The dimly lit "mock-up" consisted of fifteen radar scopes, all manned by radar men. One exception was the scope that Larry Holder had cranked down for repair. Sprawled out under it, he flashed an occasional beam of light from his flashlight up into the old electronic circuitry.

"So what do you think?" Ted asked again.

"Wake me up when the lights come on," Larry said, giving Ted a quick glance. There was nothing wrong with the scope. One of the trainees was having a problem and his officer called the "ET Shack" to report the problem. Ted and Larry checked it out and found it to be an operator error.

Being the seasoned sailor that he was, Larry saw the chance to put the scope out of service, crank the machine down, and use it as a canopy for an afternoon snooze. He took it.

"Do we have a time table on this?" a harried, young officer asked Ted.

"It's just hard to say. Probably won't have it up by 16:00. We'll do our best, sir," Ted responded. Everybody went home at 16:00 – 4:00 P.M. in the real world.

"What about tomorrow?" the officer asked.

"I'm sure we'll have it up by then."

The officer nodded and went back to monitoring the trainees work.

Ted stood by the machine for several minutes with Larry lying motionless beneath the machine. Larry's snoring prompted a slight kick in the side. An annoyed Larry looked up toward his attacker.

"You were snoring," Ted said.

"Keep up the good work, lad," Larry said as he resumed his position.

Ted stood sentry, serving Larry an occasional nudge over the next hour and fifteen minutes. At 15:45 the lights came up and the trainees filed out of the room.

Larry Holder cranked the radar repeater back to its upright position. Ted helped him put the cover back on. They walked back to the ET Shack to check out – eight more hours of undetected crime.

"You and Bobbi got plans for tonight?" Ted asked.

"I don't know.... What you got in mind?" Larry asked.

"Sam and Mike were talking about going down to the Market area and tipping a few brews," Ted said. "Probably Blackbirds around eight."

"We might see you there," Larry said with a left-handed mock salute.

"Eight o'clock," Ted said with a smile and a wave.

They went their separate ways – Ted to the barracks and Larry to his off-base apartment and his wife Bobbi.

"Thirty-eight, thirty-nine, forty.... Off the rim... too bad!" Sam Conner howled. "Hey... it was thirty-seven more than your last effort."

The event in question consisted of pitching peanuts into the air and catching them in one's mouth. The talent required for this sport was almost beyond description.

"Here you go," an irritated Ted Miller said as he handed the basket of peanuts to Sam. "What's your best effort... five wasn't it?"

"I've been laying back."

"That's obvious as hell," Ted said.

"Ooh... a sporting event. You know how I love jocks," Bobbi Holder kidded as she and Larry slid into the two vacant chairs at the table.

"Hear that, Larry. You better start pumping iron. Your wife's got the hots for us."

"What about if I pump my foot up your ass," Larry Holder responded. He was always kidded concerning his wife. Bobbi Holder was great fun and filled out a pair of jeans like most women could only hope for. Anyway, she was in love with her husband.

"Are you boys gonna fight over me again?" she smiled as she sipped on the tall draft in front of her. "I love these Navy towns."

"I bet you do," Larry said, giving her a sly look.

"And this is?" Sam asked, looking up as Seaman Mike Mason stepped to the table with a stunning brunette at his side.

"Ladies and gentlemen, this is Estelle Pasko.... Estelle, these are my friends and partners in crime."

"My pleasure," she smiled at the group.

Mike Mason was one of those guys who ended up with the women. His nice guy routine and good looks always paid dividends.

"Estelle tells me of a hot party tonight at her uncle's house... plenty of free beer and food... right up our alley."

"What will your uncle think of a car load of sailors crashing his party?" Larry asked.

"I don't see anybody in uniform.... He wouldn't care anyway. Let's go," she said.

*   *   *   *

The party was a riverfront affair at the residence of a Mr. Harone Pasko. It was a rollicking gala with two hundred people in attendance. The Naval revelers settled in for whatever the evening might bring.

Several beers into the evening, Estelle showed up at their table with a man in his early thirties at her side.

"I would like you to meet my uncle, Marko. He's in the golf business. He might have a business proposition for you when your Navy days are through," she said.

"The girl doesn't beat around the bush, does she?" Marko Pasko noted. "Thank you, darling," he said waving her off. "I am looking for a few special people for a project I have going on in Myrtle Beach.... Estelle tells me you'll be out of the Service in a few months."

"That's right," Larry said. "We get out within two months of one another. What kind of work are we talking about?"

Marko swished the drink in his hand. "I own a successful golf course in North Myrtle Beach, Droughbrigh Country Club." He went on carefully. "I am considering going in another direction with the course. I need people who are loyal and willing to take chances. The work will consist of normal golf maintenance – small repairs, grounds work, mowing. Of course I can get anyone for that kind of work.... No, I'm looking for people with other skills. People who want more and want compensated accordingly. Someone who is willing to take chances."

Marko had gotten the attention of the table. They wondered what he was getting at.... He continued. "I need specialized work... twice per month - the first Saturday and Tuesday of each month." He stopped and studied the group. "What do you think of grass... and I don't mean the kind you mow?" he abruptly asked.

A slow grin came on the faces around the table. "Is it that obvious?" Bobbi asked with her sultry smile. They had been high all evening.

Marko cast her an admiring glance her way. "I need several people to help me smuggle grass. It will be delivered to the golf course on Saturday and sent out on Tuesday. Your pay would be extraordinary, fifty plus to start."

The number surprised the table. The most they could hope for when they got out of the Navy would be fifteen or twenty thousand a year. This guy was talking fifty, all for taking a few chances.

"I'm talking long term," Marko went on, sensing that the table was interested in the proposition. "Steady work, relatively easy work, great pay... a few chances, yes.... The question is, are you interested?"

"What if we're not?" Larry asked.

"Then we've got a problem," Marko said.

They looked at each other around the table. This just might be the break they were looking for.

Larry Holder finally said, "I think it's worth talking about."

Marko Pasko smiled and ordered drinks all around. They talked into the night.

*   *   *   *

"They're waiting for you," Barney said when the large panel truck pulled up to the gatehouse. Barney Albright had manned the club gate every Saturday for eleven years. He moved to North Myrtle ten years ago from the Richmond area. Like so many retirees, his income needed a little help. Droughbrigh Country Club provided just that. Barney was clueless about the real business the panel truck was bringing to the club. *Good boys*, Barney thought as he waved them through.

The Porter Transport truck pulled through the gate and took the same path that it had traveled for years. The driver's name was John Browner. He had been the only driver on the run for nine years. Browner was a large man with high blood pressure and very little personality. He made good money and the truck afforded him a good view of the ladies on the highway.

Marie's husband, Sam, was watching for the truck from the ridge above the barn. "Here he comes," Sam relayed, via radio, to Larry, who was still sitting at the card table.

Larry motioned for Ted to press the automatic door button, and the large rollup door squeaked its way up. Larry's wife, Bobbi, directed the truck as it backed in. John's admiring eyes watched her in his mirror. Ted, Marie, Mike, and Larry waited behind the truck with the power lifts. Sam remained stationed on the hill to insure that they didn't have any surprise visitors. Hannah remained ready to help if needed.

"Could those jeans be any tighter?" John said just loud enough for Bobbi to hear as he stepped out of the truck.

"Go to hell, John," she said over her shoulder as she went to join the others. Bobbi didn't mind turning a few heads but John's wasn't one of them.

The rear of the truck was loaded with bags of fertilizer and grass seed. The crew expertly moved the pallets to storage bins. Ten minutes into the work they got to the real reason they were here this clear Saturday morning. Five tons of fine Colombian marijuana, fresh from the Port of Charleston, was neatly packed in fifty-pound sacks.

The shipment had been the same every month for nine years. A connection in Baltimore paid eighty dollars a pound for the grass. The proprietors of Droughbrigh Country Club had been turning a cool half million, less expenses, every month for nine years. They were netting three hundred and fifty thousand dollars per month. This added kick made Droughbrigh the greenest golf course in Myrtle Beach.

The marijuana was stashed in the back room of the barn. The storage room was a vault, for all intents and purposes. The door would open only by computer activation. The wall would spread apart and reveal a secret room twenty feet deep and the width and height of the barn.

Twenty-five minutes after he arrived, John Browner pulled back through the gate as Barney gave him a naïve waive. John's paperwork read fertilizer and grass seed just like always.

Sam watched as John drove off before joining the others in the barn.

They were all in their late twenties. Sam Conner was a slim guy who wore glasses. People with low standards could confuse him with an intellectual. He met his wife Marie on the sand at Myrtle Beach four years before. She was a good hearted, thin blond beauty, just a little bit on the flighty side. They were happy.

Larry and Bobbi Holder had been married since their navy days. He was tall and lean with a shaggy beard. She was a tall shapely brunette. Their marriage had seen better days. For the time being they were still together.

Ted Miller was a likable squatty guy. He had a few relationships along the way but nothing serious and had managed to stay single.

Mike and Hannah Mason were high school sweethearts with classic good looks. Mike had been in on the Barn operation since the early days. With their marriage, Hannah joined in early on. Mike was tall and muscular with sandy hair, while Hannah was petite with shoulder-length auburn hair and blue eyes.

With the front door secured, they gathered around the table and lit up the first of three fat joints that Sam had just rolled from their fresh new bag of grass, complements of Porter Transport. Typical jobs with other golf courses might have brought them thirty five thousand a year if they were lucky. This crowd was bringing in sixty thousand each per year. They took some chances, but their bread was being buttered quite nicely, thank you very much.

Larry took a long drag and handed it to his wife, Bobbi. Bobbi and Larry got stoned every day of their life. They were under the illusion that it was keeping them together. Maybe it was. The group smoked down two of the joints without having much to say. Mike and Hannah didn't smoke.

"This is damn crazy," Bobbi said to no one in particular. "It's only a matter of time before we get found out."

Ted stood up to stretch his legs and said, "Yeah, right.... Let's talk about something else."

"Excuse me for thinking. It's just no way to live, wondering if I'm going to be in jail next month," Bobbi said. "So you've never thought about it, right?" she said looking at Ted.

"Maybe they'll just put me in jail and you can have your party," Larry said sarcastically to her. There was probably more truth to that statement than either would care to admit. Not too many years before the thought of life apart from each other seemed foreign, not any more.

"Yeah, now you're talking," Bobbi said.

"I can't afford to leave this gig," Ted said. "None of us can."

"I can! This is no kind of life. I feel like I'm in prison," Marie said. "I'm not going to do this the rest of my life. Sam and I want to have a family. This isn't any way to bring a child into the world."

Hannah gave her a knowing nod.

Ted threw the cards that were in his hand across the room. He looked at Marie and scowled, "I wondered when this maternal crap would start kicking in. It's a big bad world out there, darling. Sometimes we got to put up with stuff we don't like. You need to grow up, for crying out loud!"

Marie's husband, Sam, wheeled Ted around and stuck his finger in Sam's face and yelled, "Don't ever talk to her that way... do you hear me?"

Ted pushed Sam to the floor, landing on top of him. His hands were tightening around Sam's neck. "You bastard!" Ted yelled. "She's got you wrapped around her finger!"

The women scattered as Larry grabbed Ted's shoulders pulling him off of Sam and throwing him up against the side of the Grounds Barn. "Knock it off," Larry snarled. "What the hell is wrong with you? She's got a right to express her opinion... Get out of here until you cool down. We ain't got no damn time for this!"

"My pleasure," Ted said as he stomped from the barn.

The past several months had seen everyone's nerves wear thin. None of them could afford to leave. The couples were hauling in $120,000 per year. The $60,000 Ted was bringing in kept him in beer and designer clothes.

Somewhere in the money and danger, their lives had become casualties. Normal was not in the cards for this crew. The dream of having a child was eating away at Marie's heart. She had to do something. Her husband Sam would support her in whatever they had to do.

They were not the only disgruntled couple. Mike and Hannah Mason were biding their time as well, waiting for a good reason to bolt. Life took on a different hue in their thirties as opposed to the view of just a few years before.

"I know," Larry said, "let's call up Marko and tell him we want out. I'm sure he and Mona would be very understanding."

They all knew that was a big joke. The Paskos had them by the throat and they knew it. They were pawns in the big game. Marko and Mona Pasko had owned the course for fifteen years. They were in their mid forties and lived on a large estate three miles due west from the club.

Marko was a large, obnoxious, arrogant, loud mouth womanizer who lived and partied hard. Mona was a tall slim woman who usually had a man on the side and always got her way, one way or the other.

"We wouldn't live ten minutes if we tried to split," Bobbi said. They all knew that was true. "How in the hell could any of us leave this, anyway? I mean, it's a great job. We sure don't work hard. It's just so damn nerve racking. Hey, we've made it nine years. Maybe we can do another nine."

"I feel like I'm their slave," Marie added. "The money is good but the price is killing me."

"You all can spend your life like this if you want to," Mike said, "but when we get our chance we are going to split. I don't care what the Paskos or you think."

"Yeah, I bet," Larry Holder said looking at Mike. "Bottom line, boys and girls, is we are going to be right here next year and no doubt the year after that. We get along, we got good grass, and we're making good money.... Hand me that damn joint."

CHAPTER 2

"OK, JAKE... YOU AND SALLY come on out and show us how it's done," Bonnie Harpon, the instructor at the Beach Dance School, said. The Saturday morning class had a better-than-average turnout.

"Why us?" Jake whispered into Sally's ear as they headed for the floor.

"She thinks you're funny," Sally said.

"I haven't said anything to her," Jake returned.

"She thinks your dancing is funny."

"Since when did 'she' get a sense of humor?" Jake mumbled.

Bonnie grabbed Jake's stiff shoulders and twisted him into position, gave Sally a "good luck" look and said, "Ok, you two, begin with this next song, one and a two and, start." She stepped back to observe with just a trace of a smile on her face.

Jake immediately started off on the wrong foot. He recovered quickly, but not quick enough to get in time with the music. Regrouping, he and Sally tried again. This time it went slightly better.

"Watch me now, one, two, three, four," Bonnie said as she went through the steps.

More embarrassed by the minute, Jake threw his hands up and walked off the floor. Sally followed.

"I can't do this, Sally. I just can't learn to dance," Jake said.

"You're gonna learn to dance, Jake Brown. We need to practice at home. You're gonna be great at this."

I could live so long, Jake thought to himself. "I need a drink!"

Jake Brown and Sally McSwain were sweethearts. They were both nearing sixty and retired, so to speak, in Myrtle Beach - Jake from the Post Office and Sally from a career in real estate. Both had deceased spouses from years before.

Jake had a part time gig going called Strand Private Eye, of which he was the CEO. His sporadic work consisted of light stuff with an occasional big surprise thrown in. Sally thought it would be a good idea if Jake learned how to dance. He was not so sure.

The dance lesson mercifully broke up after an hour and a half. Everyone promised to return the following week, some rather reluctantly.

Jake dropped Sally off at her house and headed home. Most weeks they spent a couple of nights sleeping over. The sleeping over part was not something that they had planned. It just happened.

The Meadows subdivision, off Highway 501, was where Jake called home. His trusty dog, Amos, would be glad to see him.

*　　*　　*　　*

Marko and Mona Pasko lived on the Hanslow Plantation, a massive estate five miles inland from the Atlantic and three miles directly west from Droughbrigh Country Club. They had owned the Club outright for fifteen years and had been married almost twenty.

Two years after their marriage, Mona's uncle, James, passed away leaving Mona with his entire estate. Unknown to anyone, the old man had accumulated eight million dollars in assets. With two million dollars Marko and Mona had purchased the Hanslow Plantation. Two years later they bought Droughbrigh for five million. Six years after that, Marko and his brother Harone, who owned a trucking company in Charleston, came up with their marijuana scheme. It turned Droughbrigh from a struggling, under funded, golf course, into a money cow.

The workers at the Barn, Marko and Mona, Harone and his driver, and the Marianno people were the only ones who knew what the real deal was at Droughbrigh.

The Marianno connection was a mob tie-in from Baltimore. They paid the Paskos a cool $800,000 every time they picked up a load.

The Paskos had a son named Billy. He was a pudgy smart mouth who had a knack for getting on everyone's nerves.

Gina Lacky was the maid. She was a beautiful, twenty-one-year-old, with long brown hair, model looks, and a knockout figure. Despite Marko's advances, she would not give him the time of day. It was a wonder she kept her job.

The Paskos also had in their employ a groundskeeper named Herndon Jones, a likable sixty-year-old black man who always looked at the bright side of life. Herndon was a Christian man with a constant smile on his face. He and Gina were the only "normal" people who called Hanslow Plantation home.

Saturday evening Marko, Mona, and Billy were seated at the table in the sunroom that overlooked a five-acre pond. Gina Lacky brought in the main course for the evening - a delicious salmon concoction. Where that young girl learned to cook was a mystery to everyone at the table. But learn to cook she did.

"Thank you, Gina," Mona said as Gina slipped out of the room.

Marko and Billy watched Gina as she walked away.

They ate in silence for several minutes. The Paskos were a joyless bunch.

"I gotta go into town tonight," Marko finally announced.

Mona knew he was whoring around. He loved to frequent the strip clubs and was very well acquainted with any number of local dancers.

"What, you got business?" Mona said as she wiped her chin. She knew damn well that it wasn't business. The old saying "money can't buy happiness" could not have been more clearly demonstrated than by the Pasko household.

"Yeah, business," Marko smiled with a toothy grin.

"My asshole's really been bothering me," Billy announced out of the blue.

"What's that, Billy?" Marko asked.

"My asshole... it's been bothering me."

"Call the doctor next week," he said to Mona. "His asshole is bothering him."

"I think we all have an asshole that's bothering us," Mona said not looking up from the mail she was reading.

"Does your asshole ever bother you, Dad?"

"It's been a long time, Billy. A long damn time."

Gina walked into the room. She stood next to Marko and asked, "Does anyone want dessert?"

Marko looked at her with drool on his lips. She stared back with total disgust. Mona loved the way Gina looked at Marko. She didn't pander to him at all. In fact she seemed to like pissing him off.

"What we got, beautiful?" Billy asked.

"Apple pie and vanilla ice cream," she made herself say. She tried to answer Billy with some semblance of civility even though she couldn't stand the punk. After all, he was her employer's kid.

Billy and Marko nodded their approval. Mona passed. That was why she weighed 105 pounds and the "boys" weighed considerably more.

They finished the evening meal with little additional conversation. Marko left for town shortly after dinner. Billy got on with his favorite pastime, trying to catch a glimpse of Gina in a nude or nearly nude condition. He had spy places set up all over the house. If Gina had known she would have gladly killed him.

Mona stayed upset with Marko. The womanizing was one thing, but that wasn't the whole story. He was an out-of-control thug who did what he wanted, when he wanted. He did not expect a discussion from Mona or anyone else. Any opinion that was not his own meant nothing to him. Despite his ruthless behavior, Mona usually managed to have the last laugh.

His money brought him attention. Women were always hanging around. *Like getting into the sack with Marko was going to bring them some money. That was a joke,* Mona thought.

Mona, on the other hand, was more discreet in her dealings. Early on in her marriage she found she had a knack for turning heads. Her thin sleek figure had always drawn admirers. She wore clothing that flaunted her best attributes, that being her long legs and nice rear.

Her favorite toy these days was a hunk named Monty Purcer who also happened to be her masseur. He was a muscular, dark skinned, young man, with an abundance of body hair, and good-looking features. She had been seeing him twice a week for several months. She seriously entertained the idea of life without Marko and the freedom to pursue hunks like Monty. Divorcing Marko was a very real possibility, a very lucrative possibility at that.

The drug thing complicated the picture. A messy court scene was not what she had in mind. She did not want to risk that. She had another angle in mind. She could catch him with his pants down just a few too many times. She could force him to accept a nice quiet settlement. As careless as Marko was, that wouldn't be hard to do. It was about time to get the ball rolling in that direction.

*   *   *   *

The night was still early when Marko Pasko pulled into the Stag Gentleman's Club on Highway 17. The parking lot had just a few cars in it. They waved him in and he took his place at his familiar corner table.

A new girl, going by the name of Star, was "bumping and grinding" on the stage. Marko watched the young girl with keen interest. After her set she exited the stage, said a few comments to the men on the runway, and went to the bar to get a drink. The bartender motioned her toward Marko and she jointed him at his table. Five hundred dollars and three hours later, after a romp at his townhouse, Marko returned her to the club.

*   *   *   *

Sunday morning Jake picked Sally up and headed for the Beach Deli for breakfast. She was making her first visit to one of Jake's favorite haunts. As they walked in the door, Jake had a sudden, sinking, feeling. A certain waitress was working who Jake was sure never worked on Sunday.

Jill Arthur was a good-looking, long-legged brunette of excellent proportions - a genuine heart breaker. For some unknown reason she had developed a special bond with Jake. It had to be a "father-figure" syndrome. Jake had gone to great lengths to describe to Sally how good the biscuits were, but for one reason or another, he had failed to say anything about Jill's legs. He hoped they would get another waitress. They did not.

"Well, hey, Jake. You doin alright?" Jill asked as soon as they were seated.

"Sure am. Two coffees please," Jake said.

"You better introduce me, Jake Brown," Jill said. "You must be Sally," she said looking at Sally.

"Yes I am.... And you are?" Sally asked, glancing between her and Jake.

"Jill... Jill Arthur," she said extending her hand. "Jake speaks often of you."

"Really?" Sally said. "He's never mentioned you."

Jake, seeing a need to stage a rally, said, "Yeah, Sally... Jill and I are pals."

Jill scooted off to make some coffee.

"Pals... oh that's sweet," Sally said, looking straight through him. "I think everybody needs a pal," she said with her eyes beamed like darts into Jake's helpless face.

"It's nothing really, totally innocent," he said.

"Of course it's innocent. You're old enough to be her father, for crying out loud."

"I know... that's right. I couldn't agree more."

"You do have a good-looking pal.... I'll give you that much."

"Yeah, I've always had this thing for good-looking women," Jake said with a wink.

Sally shook her head and smiled, "You can be a real ass, Jake Brown."

*   *   *   *

Jake dropped Sally off at home after church and headed home. The phone was ringing and Amos was barking when Jake walked into the house.

"Hello," he said picking up the phone.

"Is this Strand Private Eye?" a female voice on the other end asked.

"Sure is. How can I help you?"

"This is Mona Pasko. I would like to talk to you at your earliest convenience. I live in North Myrtle."

"How about tomorrow morning?" Jake asked.

"Tomorrow would be good. Would ten be ok?"

"Ten would be great," Jake said. "Where do you live?"

"I live at the Hanslow Plantation on Potter road off Highway 9."

"I know where Potter Road is," Jake said fishing for more information.

"Turn down Potter Road and it's two miles down on the left.... It's a big place on the left. You can't miss it."

"Sounds good, Ms. Pasko. I'll see you tomorrow at ten."

"It's Mrs. and I'll see you then," she said as she hung up.

Probably another domestic case Jake figured as he patted Amos's head and got himself a cola from the refrigerator. "Hanslow Plantation," he said reading his notes. "Poor people don't live on plantations anymore," he said to Amos as if the dog knew what he was talking about. It had been a few months since his last private eye work. This would be a nice diversion and he could use the cash.

* * * *

Larry and Bobbi Holder lived in a three-bedroom ranch abode three blocks off Highway 501 near the waterway. This particular afternoon found them sprawled out on the living room floor, smoking a joint and listening to music. Their usual mode was very little talk and very much smoke.

"Marie's a dumb bitch," Bobbi said to the wall as much as to Larry. "That silly damn laugh of hers gets on my nerves."

Larry took a long drag and held it in his lungs as long as he could. Five minutes later he said, "Half the time you love her and the other half you hate her. What's the deal? Sam seems to like her."

"Sam's as drifty as she is," she said taking the joint.

Larry and Bobbi's relationship had been anemic for several years. The marriage started out well, almost giddy. As the years went by the jokes got old and the laughs got fewer. Through it all they amazingly had been faithful to each other. Their job at Droughbrigh had kept them together when nothing else could have. The good drug money and the Paskos intimidation kept them showing up and hanging in.

Bobbi was an attractive girl, tall and thin with long shapely legs. She was not a flirt, but the tight jeans she preferred to wear got her plenty of opportunities. On the one hand she believed in commitment but on the other she felt trapped in a joyless marriage. Something had to give.

Larry was a calculator. Much of his time was spent figuring how they could maintain their present lifestyle and at the same time escape the grasp of the Paskos. In his misguided mindset, all their marriage trouble stemmed from their work environment. Bobbi was not under any such illusion. Larry tried dope peddling but found it too risky. Sometimes he was left holding the bag, in more ways than one. His present preoccupation was trying to figure out a way to screw Marko and Mona out of a tidy sum of money. Larry felt it was his money anyway, at least a part of it. Certainly more than they were getting paid. He and Bobbi would go to jail just like the Paskos if the gig came down.

"I've been doing some thinking," Larry said holding the joint in his hand and glancing her way. "A golfer the other day was telling me about doing business in Costa Rica. He was saying a friend of his had an online business that was very lucrative. I think it's some kind of sex business. He didn't say. Anyway, mucho money is being funneled to an account down there. The government here can't find out who holds the account and the banks down there won't tell. If he needs money he gets it from his ATM, totally undetected - no tax and totally clean."

"So?"

Larry took another long lag and bore into her with his stare. "So it just might be our answer to the Pasko problem."

Bobbi flipped her hand at him as if to say "talk to me."

He continued. "We go down to Costa Rica on our vacation and open up a private account. It would give us some leverage."

"Leverage for what?"

"Leverage for blackmail. We get Marko's password for the Barn computer. With his access we can tap into the hard drive. There's got to be plenty of stuff in there that we could use to hold their feet to the fire."

"What have you got in mind?"

Larry went on, "He keeps a lot of stuff that he doesn't want Mona to see out at the Dortshire place. We get in there and look around."

Neither one said anything. The Dortshire place was Marko's personal sex den. He used it three or four times a week usually with different women. Mona never went there. As far as they knew she didn't have a key to the place.

"So what are you saying?" Bobbi asked looking hard at Larry.

"He's always wanted to get into your pants. Take him up on it. Get him drunk, slip him a Mickey and look around while he's passed out. His password is there somewhere."

"What happens when he comes to? He's gonna be pissed."

"Not really. Just convince him that he was drunk and passed out."

"How am I going to do that?"

"You'll figure out something. You're a bright girl."

"So you want me to screw Marko?" she said looking his way. "Is this what we've come to?"

"Look, we got to do something. I ain't looking to throw everything we have away but we've got to do something. You're our ticket in there. We get the goods on them and make them pay."

Bobbi got up to get a beer. Their vacation was six weeks off. Nothing would happen before that. This plan needed some thought. She should have hated Larry for what he was asking her to do. Strangely, she did not.

*   *   *   *

Jake was on the road by nine Monday morning. A new case was always exciting. A brief stop at the Beach Deli and he would be on his way.

"I hope I didn't mess you up yesterday," Jill Arthur said to Jake as she brought him coffee and sat down across from him.

"Na, everything is cool. She's used to women making a fuss over me," Jake said with a wink.

"I didn't know I made a fuss."

"You were slobbering all over everything...It was pitiful."

"I think the drool was coming from your lips," she said.

"That obvious, huh?"

"Oh, yeah," she said, heading off to get him a biscuit.

Jake finished his breakfast and headed to Potter Road for his appointment with Mona Pasko.

Finding the Hanslow Plantation was easy enough. It was a sprawling estate with a white slab fence bordering the property along Potter Road for two hundred yards down each side of the entrance gate. Jake turned in the drive and wound his way through a moss-covered canopy and crossed two wooden bridges. Five-hundred yards from the road the drive circled back to the house.

The main house was a huge colonial structure with pillars across the front. A large fountain complemented the front of the house. Jake parked his old truck and walked up the fifteen steps to the front door. Using a huge brass doorknocker, he announced his arrival.

A pretty young woman with long brown hair came to the door and stared at Jake. "Yes?" she asked.

"I have an appointment with Mona Pasko."

"And you are?"

"I'd rather not say. It's personal and she's expecting me."

"Just a moment," she said, scurrying off.

"Mister Brown... thank you for coming. This way please," Mona Pasko said. She led him to a sitting room on the other side of the large house. Mona had short brown hair and large brown eyes. She was dressed in a long loose fitting sweater with gray tights.

"Could I offer you something to drink?" she asked before sitting down.

"No, I'm fine," Jake said.

Mona lit a cigarette and drew a couple of puffs. "Have you much experience?" she asked.

"Some... mostly small stuff. I was involved with the Liz Swanson case." Liz Swanson was a wealthy woman who was abducted some time earlier.

31

Obviously impressed with that information she asked, "How was that?"

"I was employed by her before and during her ordeal."

"Well, that's certainly some experience. I'm glad that all worked out," she said.

"Me, too."

"My situation is quite different. I need you to keep an eye on my husband. He's a notorious playboy and I want to gather as much dirty laundry on him as I can. I may need it in court."

"I'm sorry, ma'am."

"Don't be. As you can see," she said waving to her lush surroundings, "there's not much to feel sorry about."

"I guess you want pictures and the like?" Jake asked.

"Pictures, movies, witnesses, whatever we can get on the asshole."

"Is there a particular place I need to be looking?"

She drew a drag on her cigarette. "He's got a townhouse in town at Dortshire. Are you familiar with it?"

"No ma'am."

"It's at 48N, right on the water, unit sixteen. He brings bitches in there three or four times a week. I don't have a key. He doesn't want me in there. You could stake out there and get plenty of evidence. Most of the girls are dancers in the local clubs. He picks them up and takes them to the townhouse. I'm sure they're well paid."

"So you won't need me to hang around here?"

"Actually, I will need you here. We entertain a lot and he's always hitting on the women that attend. I think his success rate is quite high. We have parties and the like. He gets a lot of his contacts at those functions."

"Don't you think he might get a little suspicious with a private eye hanging around?" Jake said.... He had a tremendous grasp of the obvious.

"You will be undercover of course. I thought about passing you off as my spiritual advisor."

"Excuse me?"

"Spiritual advisor. All my friends have one."

Jake nodded his head like he understood. "You mean like your own personal priest or something?"

"No, more of an Eastern type."

"A swami?"

"Whatever... I'll let you figure it out."

"Do I need to wear a robe?"

"A robe... now that would be a nice touch. My friend's advisors don't wear robes. Yes, I think a robe would be nice, at my expense of course."

"Of course," Jake said.

"What am I supposed to do, walk around and watch the wind blow, and mutter a chant?"

"Hell, I don't know! You're the private eye, remember?"

"How am I going to explain the camera?"

"Keep it under your damn robe.... Am I going to have to do all the thinking around here? How much is this expert service going to cost me?"

"I need a thousand up front and fifty per hour plus expenses payable every week." Jake felt like a thief. He had never asked for more than two hundred dollars front money before. He was getting better at this. He was able to say it with a straight face.

"Good grief, I could have the Pope for that...whatever, I'll give you a thousand before you leave. He should give you plenty of material on a regular basis. I will expect a report, every week."

"Yes ma'am. When do you want me to start?"

"Come on Wednesday. He's usually here in the mornings. Come about nine."

"I'll be here, robe and all."
Jake saw himself to the door and rolled back into town.

CHAPTER 3

DROUGHBRIGH COUNTRY CLUB was doing a brisk Tuesday morning business. It was ladies day and there was a big turn out. Jerry Jacovey, the club pro, was teaching a group of ladies the fine points of putting. They loved Jerry. He was a tall good-looking young man with a big smile. To top it off, he was even a good guy. He was happily married, so all the flirting was harmless.

Birdie Malone was talking more than necessary. He was being paid to start people off, not talk. But talk he did. Everybody loved Birdie - the eighty-year-old retired mechanic and onetime amateur legend. Birdie loved everyday but especially ladies day.

Bob Burly was holding down the pro shop and manning the cash register. The maintenance crew was hard at work keeping up the big course.

The crew at the Grounds Barn was taking care of the delivery that came the first Tuesday morning of every month. Normally they would be working with the rest of the maintenance crew but not on the first Tuesday.

Paul Moreno of Malpass Trucking backed his panel truck into the Barn. Bobbi directed him back. Paul was a handsome mid-eastern man. Unlike the driver for Porter Transport, Bobbi liked Paul. Ray James, Paul's driving partner, was a massive black man who was pure muscle. He came along to eliminate any problems. He did a great job.

The incoming truck was filled with grass seed and fertilizer. Once the truck was emptied, the marijuana was put in the back. Several pallets of fertilizer were put back on behind it. When the transfer was complete, Paul handed Larry the envelope with a check made out to Marko Pascos for $800,000.

"How's things in Baltimore?" Bobbi asked Paul as he got ready to leave.

"Gorgeous as usual. You need to come up sometime."

"Can I leave him behind?" she said, motioning back to her husband.

"I'm not going to answer that one," he said with a wink.

On the other side of the truck, Ray was trying to make time with Marie.

"Hey baby. When you gonna sneak off with me?" he asked only loud enough for her ears.

"You better stop talking like that," she said pushing him away. "I'm a married woman you know."

"Oh, I know, honey child."

"You just behave yourself," she said as she left him standing there.

"No harm in tryin," he said to Paul as he got back in the truck. "Them some hot ladies," he said. They both laughed as the truck pulled out.

The Grounds Barn gang celebrated another successful transfer with several fat joints. Everybody was getting blitzed except Mike and Hannah. To them, life was too short to spend it stoned. The others respected them for their mindset even if they didn't say it.

"Mike's got some news," Hannah said to the red-eyed group. "Go ahead, honey."

Mike Mason shook his head in affirmation and said, "My brother called yesterday. I told you he started that advertising business up there."

"Outside of Dover?" Ted asked.

"Right," Mike went on. "Anyway, it's busting at the seams and he needs me up there. He wants me to start as soon as I can. I'll be starting out over $100,000. We got to go....We're gonna go."

The group sat in silence looking at each other and back at Mike.

"Have you talked to Marko and Mona?" Larry asked.

"Not yet...I just found out yesterday," Mike said.

"We'll be close to our parents and family...I can't wait," Hannah added.

The rest of the group stared at them.

"What...?" Hannah asked seeing the apprehension in their faces.

"They ain't gonna let you go," Marie said.

"We're not asking them, we're telling them," Mike said. "In a nice way."

The group went back to their joints. They all knew their friends were about to be disappointed.

*   *   *   *

Tuesday and Friday mornings Mona Pasko scheduled a two-hour appointment with her personal masseur, Monty Purcer, at the Stress Release Day Spa. The session consisted of a long, deep massage. Monty's exceptional good looks did not hurt his business as Mona could attest.

"I hired a private eye yesterday to get the goods on Marko. I'm going to have so much stuff on him that I could kick his ass in any courtroom in America. I'm going to do it, too. I'm tired of his bull," she said, pulling the towel around her. It was a turn on for her to tell this good-looking young guy her private business.

"When is he starting?" Monty asked.

"Tomorrow. Marko thinks he's my spiritual advisor," she said, turning to smile at Monty. "Can you believe it? I'm not putting up with his crap the next twenty years. I can tell you that."

"Got to do what you got to do, darling," he said as they stepped into the lobby.

"We'll see you Friday then, Mrs. Pasko," the receptionist said to Mona as she left. Monty went back to work with another appreciative woman.

*   *   *   *

Jake mistakenly confided in Sally that he needed a robe. In a typical female shopping frenzy, she flew into action tracking down a robe for her man. A friend told her of a consignment store on King's Highway that specialized in church apparel.

She found Jake a bright blue robe with a white star on the back. Keeping a low profile would not be an option with that garb. Jake thanked Sally for her good work. He then got into his old truck for the drive to the plantation. He practiced his chant on the way. Sally's laughing at him when he pulled away did not help his confidence.

Jake pulled into the driveway and wound his way to the front of the house. A black man of about sixty was doing some repair work to the front door.

"We done give to the Shriners," the worker said, smiling as Jake walked up. Herndon Brown, the ground's keeper and all around handy man, was more than a little amused by Jake's getup.

"Bless you, brother," Jake said looking past Herndon and into the house. "Could you tell Mrs. Pasko that Salloa is here?"

"Salloa...? Is that what you said?" Herndon asked.

"Yes sir."

"Your momma give you that name?"

"The Great Spirit gave me that name," Jake said, sensing this guy could be trouble.

Herndon almost fell over laughing when Jake said that. "Pray tell," he said. "Let me get the 'Great Mona' for you," he said, laughing as he yelled in the door. "Mona, you got company."

When she appeared, Jake kissed her hand and said, "Salloa at your service, ma'am."

Herndon snapped to attention as Mona led Jake through the front door. Herndon howled with laughter as he returned to his work.

"Where the hell did you get that damn robe?" she asked when they got out of Herndon's ear range.

"My girl friend found it for me."

"Get rid of her."

"The guy at the door might be difficult," Jake said.

"Don't worry about Herndon. He's the sanest one here," she said. "You need to meet Marko. He's out back. Don't let him intimidate you. He'll just brush you off as another one of my losing ideas... Here he comes now."

Marko walked into the room and Jake could see what she meant by intimidation. He was a large burly Greek with a face void of any kindness. When he saw Jake, he stopped dead in his tracks.

"What is that?" he said, looking at Jake but talking to Mona.

"It's a he not a what.... He's Salloa, my spiritual advisor."

"Why don't you just shred our damn money...? What the hell are you thinking?"

"All my friends have spiritual advisors and Salloa comes very highly recommended."

"Who the hell would recommend that?" he asked, while looking at Salloa with disgust.

"You have no clue about the inner person," Mona said to Marko.

Marko shook his head in amazement. He got right up into Jake's face and said, "And you think this asshole does?" Marko looked at Mona and then back to Jake. "Tell me something spiritual, meathead."

Jake gulped and raised his hands, closed his eyes and said, "I am one with earth." He continued to chant. When he opened his eyes, Marko was staring with a look on his face that resembled someone who was about to swat a fly that had just landed on his peach cobbler. He was not impressed.

He finally looked at Mona and said, "My God, Mona... has it come to this?" He stormed out of the room shaking his head.

"You did good," she said to Jake's surprise. He couldn't help but wonder what "bad" would have consisted of. "Why don't you just walk around the place and get a feel for things," she said.

Mona left and Jake meandered out the back door and headed toward a picturesque pond fifty yards behind the house. He was startled to see the maid, or cook, or whatever she was, laid out on a blanket sunbathing in a very scant bikini. They saw each other about the same time. Jake was transfixed. She pulled her sunglasses down on her nose, lifted her head and looked toward Jake with an amused look on her face. She didn't say anything, she just stared.

Not knowing what to do and quite certain that he was not looking overly pious starring at her very nearly nude young body, he gave her the "peace" sign. This broke the ice as she laid her head down on the blanket and broke into a loud laugh.

"This place is crazy," she said to anyone who would listen.

"And you are?" she asked between laughs.

"Salloa, spiritual advisor to Mrs. Pasko," Jake said, extending his hand and moving in for a closer look. He was thankful and really quite surprised that she didn't recognize him from their previous brief encounter. It must have been the robe. "And you are?"

"Gina Lacky, I'm the maid," she said propping herself up on her elbows. "Spiritual advisor, my ass.... Marko couldn't have believed that."

"He seemed to," Jake said.

"Right.... Care for a beer, swami?" she said tapping the cooler.

"Well, maybe a sip," he said helping himself to a beer. He was beginning to think that maybe she remembered him after all.

"Now tell me," she said, "are the gods pleased?"

"Pleased about what?"

"Pleased with me?"

"Yes, I would say they're quite pleased," Jake said, glancing quickly over her physique.

"So how long you been in the swami business?"

"You mean the spiritual advisor business."

"Whatever."

"The journey began fifteen years ago."

"What... you get hit in the head with a rock or something?"

Jake was surprised how quickly he drank his first beer. He got himself another one. "Actually, young lady, I had an encounter with a grand master."

"Don't tell me.... It was in Tibet, right?"

"No, actually, it was in Marion."

"Marion.... You mean Marion, South Carolina?"

"One in the same."

"Marion, South Carolina," she said with a mock smile. "How damn lovely is that?"

"What have you got against Marion?"

"Nothing against Marion," she said. "It's quite the garden spot." She got herself another beer and laid down on the blanket. Momentarily she propped herself up again and asked, "What are you really doing here? Are you screwing Mona?"

"My dear, please. I am a spiritual advisor," he said as piously as he could muster with two beers in his system. That comment brought another chuckle from Gina. She gave Salloa a wink, before placing a magazine over her eyes, and proceeded to catch some rays.

The minutes turned into hours and before Jake knew it, Salloa was drunk. Jake was known to drink an occasional beer, two at the most. Four beers on this day just tore the old boy up. Gina managed to get the drunken swami to the drive and into his truck. "Pull off the road the first chance you get and take a nap." She slammed the door and waved him on. "Get the hell out of here!" she said with a wink. Jake drove a half-mile, stopped under a tree, and passed out.

CHAPTER 4

"SO WHO ARE THEY?" Marko asked.

"La Capa Shipping. Good boys, highly recommended," his brother Harone said from a phone in his Charleston home. "They're no problem. We pay them the same as before, fifteen percent. They're good boys."

"I guess we had to do something," Marko said. "Those other assholes were drunk half the time."

"We tried to talk with them. They wouldn't listen. What could we do? The La Capa boys though are different, first class," Harone said.

"I trust your judgement, brother. I always have.... So how's the family?"

"Fine. Brenda gives her regards to Mona."

"Brenda says 'hi,'" Marko said to Mona who was sitting in a chair across from him. She flipped her hand in acknowledgment.

"She says 'Hi.' I wired the money.... You did get it?"

"Yesterday," Harone said.

"What about our friend in Bogota?" Marko asked.

"Mr. Manuel is fine. He's running for office you know."

"I didn't know that. What's Ellias running for?"

"Deputy of Police.... Can you believe it?"

"That could be helpful," Marko said in an understated tone.

"Very helpful. Yes, you could say that. His jurisdiction would include all of the Keora Valley. It will be smooth sailing indeed if he gets elected."

"What are his chances?" Marko asked.

"From what I understand, he's a lock. His competition is a woman.... Women are useful for one thing in Columbia, and it is not running law enforcement."

"Maybe they are not so backward after all, my brother," Marko laughed. "It's been nine years, Harone. We must continue to be careful. The walls have ears. They always have."

"I know," Harone said. "We're a well-oiled machine. It's taken years to get to this point. We must continue, but we must be careful. I know we will."

They chatted a few more minutes and they were off the phone. Marko sank into his easy chair across from Mona. Despite his many women, Mona still stirred his passions with her long slim lines and seductive ways. He admired her as she looked through a magazine.

He was not under any illusion concerning her faithfulness. That was shelved early on for them. In a sick kind of way their mutual indiscretions had added a certain seasoning to their marriage. They weren't with each other enough to get bored.

"And Harone is good?" she asked.

"Yes, the same. We have a new shipper, La Capa, an outfit out of Columbia. Harone says they're to be trusted." Marko arose and poured himself a drink. "Ellias may become the new law officer," he said to her surprised look. "It could be very good news for our operation. He seems certain to win the election."

"When's the election?" she asked.

"November."

"So when will you be going to Bogota?" she asked.

"February, I think it is. I'll let you know."

"That would be nice."

He studied her for a moment and began to massage her neck from behind. "I want you tonight, Mona."

She put down her magazine and arose. Marko followed her to the bedroom.

*　　*　　*　　*

"Yes," Gina said answering the door.

"Mike and Hannah Mason, the Paskos are expecting us," Mike said.

Gina led them to the back sunroom where the Paskos were waiting. Marko stood when they walked in.

After a few pleasantries, Mike went on to tell of the job offer from his brother and their plans to take the job and move to Delaware.

When he finished, Mona looked at her hands while Marko stared at his guests. He didn't say anything for several moments.

"This does present a problem," he said. "We pay you very well.... Why would you want to leave?"

"I think I've explained myself.... We just want to be with family."

Marko and Mona looked at each other. "There is more to this than just you and I. There is my brother and, of course, Malpass Trucking.... I don't think they are going to go for this."

"I'm sorry. We do appreciate everything you've done. We just got to do what we got to do," Mike said.

"We've always wanted to live near our families. My brothers and sisters need help with my parents. They're getting older."

"You have vacation time coming, go see them. I can even give you extended time if you need it," Marko said.

"That's not what we're asking," Mike said. "I'm going to take the job. I'm not asking for your permission. I'm just letting you know what our plans are. Hannah and I hold you both in high esteem. We just have to think about what's best for us for the rest of our lives."

"That's a dangerous position," Marko said. "The Marianno family will not be happy."

"We're no threat to them," Mike said. "We won't speak of the drugs to anyone. The workers at the Barn are our best friends. We would never say anything to compromise them."

Hannah nodded her agreement.

"I'm afraid they won't see it that way," Marko said.

"I can't help that," Mike said. "They will understand in time."

"You're making a mistake."

"We'll take our chances."

*   *   *   *

Mona's eyes were steady on Marko as he dialed the number. The Mason's leaving was the biggest crisis their drug business had faced. It was not just a matter of someone wanting out. It was a matter of protecting their closely-held secret operation and, more importantly, it was the security of the Baltimore Mob that could get compromised.

They had done their best to convince the Masons to reconsider but their minds were made up.

Marko described the situation to Theo Marianno who sat in his Baltimore office. When he finished there was silence on the other end.

Finally, Marianno said, "We'll handle it." He said and hung up.

Marko looked at Mona with fixed eyes. He sat in his chair and took a big swig of whiskey. They were afraid to think what those few words could mean.

* * * *

"Maybe we should call a doctor," Sally said.

"No, I'll be fine. I just had a restless night."

"Are you sure you're not sick? You look terrible." Sally said as she checked Jake for a fever.

"No, I'm fine, really," Jake said. He didn't bother telling Sally about his three hour drunk with the young and lovely Gina Lacky. He gingerly removed the icepack from his head.

"When do you go back out there?" she asked, referring to the Hanslow Plantation.

"Friday.... She wants me there Wednesdays and Fridays. Sometimes I'll have to go for special parties and the like. It just depends." About that time he caught his profile in the mirror. "God, I look awful," he said, hoping Sally would offer a "No, you don't" or something similar.... She didn't.

"How did the robe work out?" she asked.

"Probably could have toned it down just a little," Jake said.

"You think anyone was suspicious?"

"No one was suspicious," he said. "I think it went well."

"So are you done till Friday?"

"I've got to do some stakeout work tomorrow evening. There's a good chance Marko will bring a girl to his townhouse tomorrow. I need to be there with my camera ready to take pictures. I'll go early and find a good place to hang out."

"What if he sees you?"

"He won't recognize me. I won't have my robe on," Jake teased. "I'll just have to be sure that he doesn't see me.... This is 'hush-hush' of course."

"Of course," she said.

They feasted on hotdogs and beer. She spent the night and left at nine the next morning. It was just as well. He was supposed to meet his friend Joe Lane on the Third Avenue Pier.

Joe Lane was a grumpy, retired machinist from somewhere up north. He was obnoxious at best and sometimes just plain disgusting. He did have a nice wife named Jane who, despite Joe's complaining, was the best thing that ever happened to him. They had some health issues but they were happy. Joe spent half his waking hours on the pier. Jake usually joined him a couple of days a week when we wasn't "private eyeing."

The Third Avenue Pier was managed by a little man named Ralph Causey. Jake paid Ralph a few dollars to fish, bought some cut bait, and headed out. He found Joe half way out on the north side trying to coax a flounder onto his bait.

"Look what the cat drug in," he said with his big grin and looking Jake's way.

"What you say?" Jake asked, not quite understanding what Joe said.

"Pull my finger," Joe said, starting the conversation out with his only talent.

"Anything hitting?" Jake asked, ignoring Joe's finger.

"Not yet. Everybody's waiting for the spot to come in. Hasn't happened yet." Joe fished a drink out of his cooler. "Where you been?"

"I'm working again. It's a trail my old man case. The people own a golf course and I think she wants to dump him." That really wasn't confiding anything. The Myrtle Beach area has over a hundred golf courses.

"She wants to take him to the bank, huh?"

"I guess so. She wants me to follow him around."

"How long?"

"Six months, I don't know...a while."

"She figuring it's gonna take that long to get the goods on him? What is he, some kind of saint?"

"Not hardly. The goods part should be easy. She just wants a whole lot of it. In the meantime, I've got a job."

"Yeah. I know how work rubs you the wrong way. Which one do they own?"

"Sorry, confidential information."

"Maybe you can get some free golf out of this."

"I hadn't even thought of that."

"You're slipping, boy."

"Sally wanted me to see if you and Jane could come over Saturday night and grill out. Rudy's gonna be there. I think he's bringing his girl friend."

"Sure. I'm not above slumming every now and then. He's the retired cop, right?"

"One in the same."

"I won't hold it against him," Joe said.

"Good."

Jake fished for a couple of hours and went home. He needed time to get his stakeout supplies together and he wanted to be at the Dortshire Townhouse an hour before dark.

*   *   *   *

Sam and Marie Conner were off work every Sunday and Thursday. This particular Thursday afternoon found them wandering around the old river district in Georgetown.

On their days off they liked to get away. A jaunt to Georgetown was one of the easiest ways to do it because it was only forty-five minutes from Myrtle Beach and yet seemed a world away. They enjoyed walking through the old shops and looking for a bargain.

"Look at that store, Sam, 'Swamp Stuff.' Let's go in there," Marie said.

Swamp Stuff was an unusual place. The walls were covered with homemade items from the area. Most articles were made from snakeskin and alligator hides. Various practical and decorative carved wood items were everywhere in the store.

"Do you need any assistance?" a smiling black woman of about forty said to them. Osa and Holmes Chamblin owned the small downtown shop after having spent many years living in a nearby swamp. Christian music played in the background and Osa's face seemed to radiate love.

"I was just looking at this little doll," Marie said. "Did you make it?"

"Yes, I did," Osa said.

"It's beautiful," Marie said.

"Do you have a little girl?" Osa asked.

Marie looked at her with sadness in her eyes. "No," she softly said. "Maybe someday."

Osa could sense the longing in Marie's heart. "I bet God could bring you a baby.... Have you ever asked him?"

"I know I should have but I haven't," Marie said. "My situation is about impossible."

"Honey, nothing's impossible with God."

Marie was struck by this sweet woman's concern. She had not known her five minutes but already Osa spoke to her as if she was giving advice to her very own child.

"Thanks," Marie managed.... It was all she could do to keep from crying.

A large black man walked in the store holding a wooden box with a screen on the top.

"I's found two just outside of town. What you think?" Holmes said to Osa.

Sam made the mistake of looking in the box, "Watch out! There's snakes in that box!"

Marie screamed and jumped back.

"I's so sorry, missy. Holmes not mean to frighten you."

"You need to be more careful, darling," Osa said. "Take those in the back."

"Sorry. He doesn't mean any harm. You just look around. If there is anything I can help you with you just let me know," Osa said.

Sam bought a hat with a snakeskin lining for twenty-five dollars and they were on their way.

CHAPTER 5

THE DORTSHIRE COMPLEX OFF 48N was easy enough to find. It was a reasonably upscale place complete with ocean front balconies. The majority of the dwellings were time-shared out.

Jake positioned his car so his passenger side window was directly across from the front door of unit sixteen. His right-angle lens was setup on his video recorder so he could look straight ahead so as not to look suspicious and at the same time film the comings and going with a high-power telescoping lens. His camera and film setup enabled him to take movies in broad daylight or in the middle of a moonless night. The tinted glass on his windshield blocked anyone from seeing him in the car. The camera directed at the complex was barely noticeable and with any luck at all would not be noticed.

Marko's club of choice this evening was the Cadillac Club on Highway 22. One of his favorite girls, stage name "Bunny," was the featured dancer for the evening. He arrived at the club at 7:40 P.M. and twenty minutes later left with Bunny for the twenty-minute ride to the townhouse. Jake saw them pull up.

Jake filmed them from the time they got out of the car until they went in the front door. He was able to get high resolution close-up shots of both of them. Bunny was a stunning brunette in her late 20's. She was top heavy with long skinny legs. She obviously had been there before, going straight to the apartment followed by Marko.

Once they went inside Jake was able to focus the camera on the front door. The camera's sensing device would automatically begin recording when motion was detected. When they came out Jake would switch the camera to manual and film them going to the car.

They came out two and one half-hours later and went straight to the car and drove off. Jake would show Mona the film tomorrow during his scheduled visit to the plantation. He put his gear away and drove home.

* * * *

"Look at this one," Hannah said holding up a shell for Mike to see. "It's pretty."

Mike acknowledged the shell as they slowly made their way down the beach. An occasional wave made them scamper to keep from getting their feet wet on this mid October day.

"I'm gonna miss this place," Hannah said. "We will come back won't we?"

"We'll always come back here," Mike said. "Who knows? We might even retire here."

"I think I would like that," Hannah said. She stopped and looked across the broad expanse of the Atlantic. They both stopped and were caught up in the awesome sight before them. She turned to face him looking into his eyes.

"Are you afraid?"

He didn't want to say "yes" even though he was afraid. They had made up their mind to go. She needed him to be strong. "I'm not afraid....I know we have to be careful, but I'm not afraid."

"Do you think those Marianno people are Mafia?" she asked.

"I doubt it, but I don't really know."

"Maybe we should just go, just leave now," Hannah said. "We could stay with Mom and Dad until we find a place."

Mike stroked the hair from the eyes of his pretty wife. "We'll go soon. I promise. We'll put in our half a day next Thursday and leave at noon. A week from now we'll be in Delaware."

"I can't wait," she said as she clung tightly to her man.

*   *   *   *

Jake, complete with his blue robe with the big white star on his back, pulled up to the Hanslow Plantation at exactly noon. Marko had just arrived after morning business at Droughbrigh. Mona was leaving before long for her Friday appointment with her masseur. Jake rang the doorbell and Gina came to the door.

"Swami," she said with a smile.

"It's Salloa."

"Of course, Salloa, come on in. I'll get Mona. Have a seat."

Jake took a seat in a large club chair and waited for Mona. Marko came storming through the house looking for something.

"Mona," he yelled on the run. "Have you seen those trucking papers?" He stopped in his tracks when he saw Jake. "What the hell are you doing here?" he asked Jake as Mona walked in.

"Salloa, how are you this morning?" she said, giving Jake an "out" and Marko a dirty look. Marko turned and stormed out of the room.

"So far so good, and you?"

"Fine. Do you have anything for me?" she asked.

"Prime film footage," he said, trying not to speak too loud. "Quite incriminating."

"At the townhouse?"

"Yes. I would guess she was a dancer, young brunette, very well endowed. I've got my camera in the car. If we had some privacy, we could watch it."

"Don't worry about that now. We need to just keep gathering evidence. I didn't see you when you left Wednesday. Did you find your way around ok?"

"Yes. I had a nice conversation with Gina. Very nice girl." *Good thing she didn't see me drunk,* Jake thought.

"Yes, she is...I'll be going into town, soon. I won't be back until after five. You will probably be gone. If I don't hear from you before then, I will see you again on Wednesday. Film tonight and Monday. He'll probably show up at the townhouse.... How much do I owe you this week counting today?"

"I was here three hours Wednesday, I staked out the townhouse for three hours yesterday, and I'll be here four hours today. That's ten hours at fifty per hour... five hundred," he said.

She handed him a check for five hundred dollars and told him to keep up the good work. This was the easiest money he had ever made.

"Oh... is there any way I can get a discount at the golf course?" Jake asked. He was getting shameless in his old age.

Reaching into her purse she pulled out a card and handed it to Jake. "This card will be good as long as you're working for me. Just call the pro shop. If they're not busy you and a partner can play free." She looked at Jake and smiled. "Anything else I can do for you? How about a little blood?"

"No thanks, this is a gracious plenty."

She gave him a "Let's hope so look" and asked, "Have you met Billy yet?"

"No... and Billy would be?"

"He's our son. You will see him around. He didn't go to school today. He said he was sick."

"I hope he's alright."

"I'm sure he'll survive."

"I'm looking forward to meeting him."

She gave him a "if you say so" look and went about her business.

It didn't take Jake long to find Billy. He stepped out the back door and saw Billy sitting on the steps of the porch. The unmistakable smell of marijuana filled the air. Jake was sure he was smoking a joint. Billy quickly flicked it somewhere when Jake stepped out.

"You must be Billy," Jake said walking toward him.

"And let me guess... you're Jesus Christ?"

"I'd say that's a little irreverent wouldn't you?" Jake said. "My name is Salloa. I'm your mother's spiritual advisor."

"Spiritual advisor my ass. That's a joke. Seems to me she might have tried going to church before she hired you."

A good point, Jake thought. *The boy has some brains, despite his present altered state.* "People take different approaches when it comes to things from above," Jake said.

"Did she make you wear that thing?"

"You mean the robe?"

"Yeah, the robe, dumb ass."

"It's Salloa, young man. And no she didn't make me wear it."

"If you're trying to impress people with it I would try something else."

"Thank you, I'll keep that in mind. So, your mother tells me that you aren't feeling well today. I take it you're feeling a little better now."

"Funny how that works," Billy said.

Billy Pasko was a smart kid and did possess a certain amount of potential. It was just as obvious that he was going nowhere at the moment.

"Where do you go to school?" Jake asked, trying to get a little rapport going. Billy didn't say anything. "Is your school in the city or county?" There was still no response. Billy was not in the talking mood.

Seeing that the conversation was going nowhere fast he decided to move on. "Well, it's been sweet, Billy. I will be around for a couple of more hours if you need to talk."

"Yeah, and if I need a hole in my head I'll be sure to let you know," the brat said.

Jake smiled and happily left Billy to do whatever Billy did. Jake didn't want to know. He walked around the house and saw Herndon Jones working in the tool shed repairing a riding lawn mover. Jake walked on over.

"Hey there," Jake said. "How are you this fine day?"

"Fine, thank you very much.... Salloa wasn't it?" Herndon said with his broad contagious smile.

Jake was encouraged that someone remembered his name. "That's right, and you are?"

"Herndon... Herndon Jones," the large black man said, extending his hand.

"My pleasure," Jake said.

Herndon cleaned up his mess and walked to a nearby refrigerator. "Care for tea?"

"That would be nice," Jake said as they both took a seat in the shade of the building.

"I like the robe. Where did you get it?"

"My girl friend, I mean a friend got it for me."

"You did say girlfriend?"

"Of course."

"Just no sex?" Herndon said, looking at Jake for a reaction.

"My belief is that sex can bring one to a deeper conscience."

"You mean sex with your girlfriend, not your wife?"

"Yes," Jake said. He could see he was getting in deep.

"What religion are you?" Herndon Jones asked.

"I believe in the great enlightenment. The cosmic oneness we all share." Jake was impressed. He thought he sounded pretty good.

"Oneness with what?"

"Oneness with everything."

"Am I one with this lawn mower or am I one with the dog... one with what?"

"You are one with God."

"So that makes us God. Is that what you're saying?"

"No. We are one with God. We are not God."

"Well, if we are one with God then we are equal to God. To be one with anything means we are connected with God in some kind of shared way. At least in that regard we must be equal to God."

"That is one way to look at it," Jake said.

"If we are equal to God then we must be God. What else could be equal to God? By definition we would have to be God." Herndon was making one good point after another. Jake was not prepared to defend his made-up theology. That fact was a wonder in itself. After all he was supposed to be a spiritual advisor. It would be nice if he had an answer or two ready to deliver. Certainly there would be questions, especially from this guy.

"I sense that you are in touch with your God," Jake said.

"That's right, Salloa. The God with a capital G."

"Capital G, I don't understand."

"You know, the real God. The God of the Bible."

"The Bible. That's a nice book, a little outdated, but nice." Glancing toward the heavens, Jake was glad to see that it was a cloudless day – a little less likely that God would strike him dead.

"Outdated? How could God be outdated?"

"I said the Bible was outdated."

"The Bible is God's word. How could it be outdated?"

Jake could see that he wasn't going to win a theological argument with Herndon so he changed the subject. Jake actually believed the way Herndon did though he was not near the apologist that Herndon was. For the time being, he had to play dumb. He was doing a great job.

"How long have you worked here?" he asked him.

"Been here eight years. It's been a good job... I'm retired Army. I took this to have something to do."

"What do you think of the Paskos?"

"They've been good to me. I pretty much work when I want to. I have no complaints."

"What about Billy?"

"That boy needs a close encounter with a hickory stick."

"It might be a little late."

"I think it would still get his attention."

"How long has Gina been here?"

"She's been here about a year and a half. She cracks me up."

"How's that?"

"She just does her own thing. The only ones she treats decent are Mona and myself. Marko and Billy both have the hots for her and she won't pay them no mind. I think Mona gets a kick out of that."

"So she's probably still working here because Mona likes her?"

"That's my guess."

Jake talked with Herndon for another hour or so then chatted a moment with Gina and left for the day.

CHAPTER 6

THE SATURDAY NIGHT COOKOUT at Jake's place in the Meadows development was going well. His trusty canine, Amos, was excited because this kind of gathering always meant at least one hot dog or hamburger would end up on the ground. Someone might even slip the poor dog a bite or two.

Sally was dolled out in a cute jump suit that showed off her finest feature, that being her legs. She was having a blast. Rudy Rogers, a recently retired police officer from the Myrtle Beach Police Department and Jake's best friend, brought his new girl friend, Nita. She was in her late forties and probably of Indian decent. She was very social and quite good looking. Joe Lane, Jake's fishing pal, was being his usual crusty self. His sweet wife, Jane, was kept busy pulling Joe's foot out of his mouth.

Though surrounded by a bunch of good-looking women, the men found it necessary to crowd around the grill and watch as Jake maneuvered the hot dogs and hamburgers. They watched with keen interest as if it took actual talent to accomplish the task.

"How did a nice guy like you end up with a friend like Jake?" Joe asked Rudy.

"I was going to ask you the same thing.... I guess I'm just not that picky," Rudy said.

"You had to be a little picky when it came to her," Joe said pointing toward Nita. "Is it true what they say about Indian women?"

Rudy gave him that "What are you talking about?" look.

"You know what I mean... in the sack," Joe said.

"You want to stick this up his ass or do you want me to?" Jake asked Rudy, waving his spatula toward Joe.

"I'll let you do it, but finish my burger first," Rudy said.

It would be nice to report that the conversation raised the bar as the night went on, but that would not be accurate. In fact, it got worse.

The party broke up at midnight with everyone promising to get together soon. Jake made arrangements with Rudy to play golf at their new favorite place, Droughbrigh County Club.

*   *   *   *

The late-model sedan pulled to the gate of Droughbrigh Country Club in the early predawn hours on a cool October morning. The provided key opened the lock on the stout chain that secured the gate. The security system had been deactivated as the vehicle eased through undetected. Once inside, a call was made and the system was reactivated from a remote location. The car was parked discreetly in the back overflow lot. The occupants headed for their appointed location. A call was made and another system was deactivated then reactivated.... They waited.

*   *   *   *

Hannah and Mike Mason pulled into the gate Thursday morning at 7:00 A.M. just as they did every Thursday. Thursday morning was the one- day of the week they had the Barn to themselves. Once relieved at noon they were done for the day. Thursday mornings were usually slow and it was a time they enjoyed. They always had something planned for the rest of the day.

They had something planned for this Thursday afternoon, too. This time, however, they were not planning for a few hours but for the rest of their lives. Their bags were packed and they were ready to load up and go once they got off work. They were headed for Delaware to take the job offer from Mike's brother. They were both excited and scared.

"I'll be glad when this day's over and we're on the road," Hannah said as the car came to a stop in the maintenance parking lot two hundred feet from the Barn.

"Me too," Mike said patting her hand before getting out of the car.

It was a clear but cool morning as they approached the Barn.

Mike opened the door, deactivated the alarm system, and they both stepped through the door.

Remee, a Marianno family heavy, and two of his cohorts were waiting inside with guns drawn. They were undetected in the shadows behind the door.

With cat-like swiftness, the two thugs grabbed Mike and pushed him to the middle of the Barn. At the same time Remee spun Hannah around and stuck his deadly gun in her face. She only had time to gasp before he pulled the trigger. The impact dropped her to the floor like a sack of flour.

"No, Hannah!" Mike screamed. "You bastards!" he managed before they put the rope around his neck. They wrapped his fingers around the gun that had killed his wife and threw it to the floor next to her. The thugs placed Mike on the chair and kicked it out from under him. He gurgled and twitched as his neck was snapped, leaving him to stare unblinkingly into the darkness of the windowless maintenance barn.

* * * *

"I just opened the door...and I saw him...and then I saw her," Ted told someone for what seemed like the umpteenth time. Ted Miller was the first one on the scene at the Barn. He walked into hell at 11:50 A.M. Thursday morning.

The building was surrounded by seven police cars and a crime lab van. Radio, TV, and several newspapers from Wilmington to Charleston were there to cover the story. The police were calling it a classic case of murder suicide. The place had been dusted for prints and nothing had come up. There were no suspicious people reported on the course. The course security system had not sounded an alarm. It seemed cut and dry.

The Barn workers stood in a small circle in disbelief. Their eyes contained both deep sadness and gripping fear. It all pointed to murder suicide but none of the workers believed it. Out of fear and self-preservation they would not voice their doubt. The biting reality of what it meant to buck Marko and Mona Pasko, but more specifically Malpass Trucking, put a chill in all of their spines. If there was ever any doubt what their business partner was like, there was no doubt now.

Mona and Marko were on the scene shortly after twelve. They were both visibly shaken. Mona was white as a sheet. It was obvious they didn't do the deed. Their innocence, however, was another matter.

* * * *

The next several weeks proceeded along as best they could. Jake continued to spy on Marko on Monday, Thursday, and Friday nights. Marko always had women with him and two out of the three nights usually produced new women. Jake continued to parade his "spiritual advisor" sham at the Hanslow Plantation. The kid was a pain and the maid still occasionally sunbathed, much to the good reverend's delight. Mona's biweekly massage sessions were scheduled like clockwork. Herndon kept debating with Jake about the things of God, further revealing Salloa's spiritual ignorance. The dance lessons continued every Saturday afternoon. Jake was diagnosed with terminal "Left Foot" syndrome.

The marijuana from Porter Transport came in as scheduled the first Saturday in October and was picked up the following Tuesday morning. Larry and Bobbi Holder planned their jaunt to Costa Rica. Recent events further cemented Larry's desire to get out of the trap they found themselves in.

Larry took a drag on his joint as he studied the web page of "Domingo Bank" in San Jose, Costa Rica. "Privacy and Security" were highlighted on the ad. "International Accounts Welcomed" also caught Larry's eye.

Something had to give in Larry and Bobbi Holder's life. Every hour of Larry's day was spent under the influence of grass or alcohol. Their social life consisted of work and grass.

Larry and Bobbi's relationship had gone from bad to worse. Larry had gotten to the point that he didn't care if Bobbi had a fling with Marko or anyone else. At least he didn't think he cared. She had plenty of admirers. That was apparent wherever they went. Marko had been after her for a long time.

At one time their relationship had been healthy. The past several years and especially the last few months had seen it go south. Larry never made an effort to change things and Bobbi had long since quit trying. She needed more than Larry was willing to give. Maybe a fling would bring things to a head. At this point they didn't have much to lose.

Bobbi was to find Marko's password for the Barn computer stashed away somewhere in the townhouse. The password would allow them access to files concerning the details of the drug business. The files would give them more leverage for their blackmail scam. Once they found it, they would have to be very careful.

Marko certainly had safeguards built into the computer. He'd hired a top Wilmington security outfit the year before to be sure that the system was state of the art. The stout system was a strong reason the police determined that Mike and Hannah's deaths were murder suicide. As far as the police saw it, no one could have gotten in there ahead of them.

Bobbi was strangely silent about the whole thing with Marko. Her silence told Larry plenty. It was apparent that she wasn't dreading it. That reality, even though he acted like it didn't matter, was eating at Larry's insides.

The plan was to leave for Costa Rica on the twenty-fifth of October by way of the Bahamas. The Bahamas trip would not raise suspicions because it was one of their favorite places. They had visited there a couple of times before. Once there, they would book a flight for San Jose. In Costa Rica, they would do their banking business and return to Freeport for the trip home.

Bobbi would give Marko the "come on" at the Christmas party held every year at the plantation. Hopefully she would not need too many visits to the townhouse to find what she needed. At least that was what Larry was thinking.

"We should be able to get our air fare tickets for a little less than fifteen hundred," Larry said to Bobbi, whose eyes were fixed to the TV. She just nodded her head.

"Cheer up. You're gonna get a new boyfriend soon."

She didn't say anything.

"It ain't bothering you that's for damn sure," Larry said.

"Why don't you just drop it," she said.

Larry scratched his head and lit the joint.

* * * *

Jake had known Jill Arthur for three years. She had long black hair and gorgeous legs. She sat down across from him as he gobbled up a sausage and egg biscuit.

"What if we'd met thirty years ago, Jake?" she said with a smile and a surprisingly serious look on her face.

"That is a nice thought... especially if you were thirty instead of five," Jake said. "How's that boyfriend treating you?"

"You mean Raymond? He treats me nice. We have a good time together."

"What's it been, a couple of months?"

"Almost three months.... Closing in on a record."

"Is he local?"

"He's from Maine. I guess he got tired of the woods."

"Yeah, that Daniel Boone routine gets old after a while. So is it serious or what?"

"Not at this point.... Probably won't happen."

"Why is that?"

"Some people aren't lucky in love."

"Just because I won't let you into my pants doesn't mean that somebody else won't. I'm saving myself," Jake kidded - probably the biggest lie he ever told.

Jill got up and swatted his bald head with a dish towel. "You're a mess, Jake Brown," she said with a chuckle. She went about her work and Jake finished his breakfast.

* * * *

67

The Pasko's flight was thirty minutes late arriving in Dulles. Remee, a heavy, a driver, and a collector for the Marianno syndicate in Baltimore met them at the airport. His recent trip to Myrtle Beach was unknown to Mona. He shook Marko's hand and hugged Mona with his hand sliding discreetly down her back. It had been there before.

Mona smiled and whispered, "Hey, Remee."

Remee loaded their bags into the trunk of the SUV and began the one-hour drive to the Marianno's Maryland estate. Light rain doused the picturesque countryside as they left the city's congestion behind.

The Paskos made the journey to the DC-Baltimore area twice a year mostly to placate Theo Marianno. He expected them to pay homage. Besides, Theo Marianno enjoyed looking at Mona. All he had done was look. He hadn't been as lucky as Remee, a fact that Remee would never divulge.

The rain stopped as Remee pulled to the front of the Marianno mansion. He opened the front door for them and led them into the parlor where he left them as he went to get the Mariannos.

Theo and Ophelia both had extended pedigrees in organized crime. The Marianno family had long been the dominant crime family in the Baltimore area. Ophelia was the daughter of a DC banker with long-time Mob ties and plenty of old money.

The traditional Marianno family business had centered on drugs, prostitution, and gambling. With the popularity of the Internet much of the business had been shifted to that venue. Their profits skyrocketed with the online business and so had their customer base. At one time, the client base consisted of the seedier element that frequented the neon-lit, all-night dives, but had since shifted to the upper middle class and the posh homes of Chevy Chase and beyond.

Theo and Ophelia were in their sixties. He was a rough man with shifting eyes. She, though gracious and outwardly kind, would slit your throat if you messed with her money. Any number of people would testify to that fact if they still could.

Ophelia came into the foyer followed by Theo. Marko raised himself from the chair and kissed her hand. "Ophelia, lovely as usual," he said.

"Marko," she said. "Mona.... Did you have a good flight?"

"Very nice, a little late, but nice. Remee was waiting for us. We got through town quickly.... Theo...so good to see you," she said, hugging him and kissing his neck.

"Lovely Mona.... Marko, you're a lucky man," he said, shaking Marko's hand.

"In many ways I am, and so are you."

"Enough talk," Theo said. "I'm sure you want to freshen up. Join us in the sunroom at five for cocktails before dinner."

The Paskos excused themselves and went to their two thousand square foot suite complete with Jacuzzi, wet bar, and waterbed.

An hour and a half later the Paskos joined the Mariannos in the sunroom. Business would be discussed.

Theo lit his cigar, drew a deep drag and blew the smoke into the air. Ophelia had a slight smile as she sat across from Marko and Mona. She had that "Mona Lisa" look complete with a dagger.

"We need to get down your way sometime," she said, looking at Mona.

"Come on down. We would love to have you," Mona said.

"I would love to take in a show or two," Ophelia said.

"Let me know when you're coming. I'll get the tickets."

"Tell me, Marko," Theo said, "What is the deal with this new shipper we have from Columbia?"

"They're first-class boys, Theo. My brother has personally checked them out. They're very reliable and can be trusted."

"How do you know that?"

"My brother tells me…"

Theo cut him off. "You're brother tells you? How does your brother know?" Theo Marianno took another long drag on his cigar. Caution was a way of life for him. Crime had been the family business for decades and every law enforcement agency on the East Coast knew it. Marko Pasko was a cautious man, but compared to Theo Marianno he was a rank amateur. "Has anyone in Columbia checked their credentials?"

"I don't know, Theo," Marko said.

"What was the name again?" Theo asked.

"La Capa Shipping."

"My people will check. We must be certain, Marko."

"Of course."

"Such an unfortunate incident, murder suicide, a terrible thing," Theo said with amazing sincerity. "How are your people holding up?"

"They're doing alright. Shaken but alright," Marko said, looking oddly at the cold-blooded killer who would not hesitate to give him the same treatment.

"These things happen," he said, waving his hand in a shrugging manner…. "How did you manage getting such an attractive wife?" Theo asked Marko, casting his lusting eyes toward Mona. Ophelia had long gotten used to Theo's brash ways. Mona smiled his way. She enjoyed being the object of men's desires, even one as crude as Theo Marianno.

"I could say the same to you, my friend," Marko said diplomatically, looking toward Ophelia who gave Marko a "thank you" look.

"To our beautiful wives," Theo said, raising his glass for a toast that they all joined in on.

"We have good news coming from Bogota," Marko said to Theo as Ophelia listened closely. "Our friend Ellias Manuel is about to become the law in all of the Keora Valley. He is the favorite in the coming election for 'Deputy of Police.' We'll have the pick of the best marijuana in the Valley."

"When's the election?" Theo asked.

"November twentieth. His opponent is a woman.... She's not even good looking," Marko said as both men laughed. The women were not amused.

"It might be a good time to step up our shipment," Theo said. "Can you handle an increase from your end?"

"I don't see a problem. We could probably double it from our end." Mona opened her eyes wide with that statement.

"We need to do it," Theo said, knocking the ashes from his cigar. "How are your people doing? You have five workers, right?"

"Yeah. We have five working the Barn. They're doing fine. In nine years we haven't had any trouble."

"They can be trusted then?" Theo continued as he blew more smoke. "They might want a bigger take once the stakes go up. The bigger the payoff the bigger the problems. Increased risk for the same money does not make for happy campers."

"A raise won't be a problem," Marko said. "Right now they're making sixty each. I could double that. That should keep them sitting tight."

"You got the two couples and the dude. Is that right?"

"That's right."

"Fine looking women, I do remember that," Marianno said without acknowledging the two women in the room.

"I hire only the best, Theo. You should know that by now." Marko figured it was only a matter of time when those two girls would mean more to him than just being employees. If he hadn't needed them in the drug scam, it would have been "put out or get out" a long time ago. Marko would bide his time. After all, he was holding the cards.

"When the election is over, we need to go ahead and step the shipment up. When can you go to Bogota?"

"I was planning on going down in February."

"I want you going before that. Can you go the first part of December?"

Marko looked at Mona and shrugged, "Sure."

Theo noticed Mona looking at Marko. "Is there a problem, Mona?"

"No problem, Theo. I won't be able to make the trip. Marko will be fine without me." She had a rendezvous in mind that could keep her occupied.

"Are you sure, my dear? A woman your age needs so much attention," Theo said with a lustful laugh. "If there is anything that I could do?" With that statement Ophelia did give him an ice-cold stare. Mona and Marko ignored the comment.

"Marko, ride with me into the city this evening after dinner. I have some business to conduct and you can see some of my operation."

"My pleasure."

"Mona, will you be all right this evening?" Theo asked.

"Yes. I will be fine. I believe I will do some reading and retire early."

"Very well then," he said.

After dinner Theo and Marko went to one of the Marianno's many clubs. Mona went straight to her room and called Remee's cell phone.

CHAPTER 7

BOB BURLY LOOKED CLOSELY at the pass handed to him. "Where did you get this?" he asked with more than a little suspicion.

"I'm doing some work for Mona Pasko. She gave it to me. You might call it a side benefit," Jake said.

"It must be nice.... Sign here.... Cart number 20," Bob Burly said. Normally the green fee for Droughbrigh Country Club for late October was seventy-five plus. "You going to be working for her for awhile?" he asked.

"Maybe six months.... It's hard to say. I'm sure you'll be seeing us out here quite often."

"I'm sure," Burly said. Jerry Jacovey walked into the clubhouse. "This is our pro, Jerry Jacovey. He's the best in the Beach."

"Please to meet you, gentlemen," Jerry said, extending his hand. "And you are?"

"Jake Brown."

"Rudy Rogers."

"My pleasure men. If you need any instruction let me know. I'm sure I can work you in."

Jake and Rudy stopped for a cheeseburger and coke at the grill before heading out to the course. A shapely and heavily made-up redhead named Ginger fried up their order. She looked like she had been poured into her blue jeans. She certainly helped out in promoting memberships. She was probably included with weekend packages and was great at parties.... She even made a mean cheeseburger.

They finished their meal and headed for the course. They were met by Doughbrigh's famous "starter," Birdie Malone. In his youth Birdie was the premier amateur golfer on the East Coast. But that was years ago. Birdie had not seen par in twenty-five years - not that it mattered. Everybody loved Birdie. He was the ideal public relations man for the golf course and was paid well for it. Every course at the Beach wanted his services.

"Gentlemen," Birdie said with a smile as big as Jake's handicap. "You're next. About ten minutes." Birdie had a way of looking at you like he had known you all his life. "Where you two from?"

"We're locals. First time out here, nice course," Rudy said.

"We think so," Birdie said. "A word of advice, boys. Lay up on number two.... That water will eat ya up."

"Whatever you say, old timer," Jake said. Birdie tipped his hat and they teed off. They hit their balls in the drink on number two.

"This place is alright," Rudy said somewhere on the front nine. "I wonder what they charge the paying customers around here?"

"There was a guy in front of me from New York. He shelled out seventy dollars."

"Ouch!" Rudy said.

"It's nice, but I don't know if it's that nice."

The terrible murder at the club was not mentioned. Most people in Myrtle had heard about it. It had occurred several weeks earlier. Myrtle Beach was not immune from the ills of society. One-hundred-and-fifty-thousand people called it home even during the winter. With that many people, things did happen.

They scooted around the perfectly manicured course in just under four hours. Rudy checked in with a "Mulligan" aided ninety-six and Jake a ninty-eight. They stopped at the Beach Deli on the way home and reminded Jill how much they loved her.... She was touched.

* * * *

Larry and Bobbi Holder caught a flight out of Charleston Friday evening headed for Freeport, Bahamas. Upon arrival they booked a week's stay at a casino hotel. They spent Friday night in Freeport. The next morning they put a "do not disturb" sign on the door, caught a cab to the airport, and booked a flight to San Jose, Costa Rica.

San Jose was a bustling town of three-hundred thousand. The Costa Rican people, known as Ticos, looked European and were extremely friendly. They were some of the most courteous people that Larry and Bobbi had ever met.

It was hot in Freeport but worse in San Jose. They took a cab downtown and checked into a third floor suite at the "La Plaz Hotel." Their room overlooked the town-square - the obvious center of activity on any given Saturday night. A marimba band played away at a gazebo in the middle of the square. A thousand revelers celebrated another Saturday night dancing to the pulsating Latin beat.

Larry called room service for a pitcher of daiquiris. They drank most of it down and finished it off on the street.

The main activity on any Saturday night in San Jose was flirting. The Holders wandered around the square for an hour or so and moseyed back to their room for the night. Ironically, it was one of the best nights Larry and Bobbi had spent together in years. Ironic when considering what the not too distant future held.

Breakfast at the hotel Sunday morning consisted of a local bean and fried rice concoction known as 'Gallo Pinto." It was served up with a couple of eggs. The Holders planned a day of looking around and taking it easy. Their business would commence Monday morning.

The banking district was within walking distance of their hotel. Several banks looked promising, especially one called "Domingo Bank." The large "Foreign Investment Specialist" sign conveniently written in English got their attention. They noted that the bank opened at nine on Monday. Larry remembered seeing the bank on the Internet.

The rest of the day was spent shopping and haggling with the locals trying to save a few colons, the local currency, on souvenir items. They dined at a nearby café and drank a harsh clear drink called guaros, which supposedly came from sugarcane. It was cheap and packed quite a wallop. They mingled through the square that evening and listened to a sombrero-covered quartet. It was the kind of pleasant day that was commonplace in the early years of their marriage. Of late days like these were few and far between.

*   *   *   *

The Domingo Bank was doing a bustling Monday morning business as Larry and Bobbi walked into the foyer. Stopping at the help desk they were met by a dignified middle-age lady from Des Moines named Mildred.

"We are interested in information concerning opening an account," Larry said.

"Yes, of course," she said in perfect corn-belt English. She punched a number on the phone and smiled as they all waited.

"Buenos dais," Manuel Dalca said with a warm smile as he extended his hand. He was a man of fifty with graying hair and small dark glasses. "You are interested in opening an account?"

"Yes, we are," Larry said.

"This way, please," he said, leading them into his office.

They were served coffee that wasn't very good. Evidently the Colombian stuff didn't make it to Costa Rica.

"Americans?" he asked.

"Yes. South Carolina," Bobbi said. Manuel, though quite professional, could not help but occasionally glance at Bobbi's legs. She was not bashful about showing them off. Latin guys had a thing for legs, she was finding out. This was her kind of place.

"We have many depositors from the United States. Some of them live in the area; many do not. It is inconsequential. What kind of account are you interested in: savings, checking, investment?" he asked.

"We need something we can access from outside the country but not necessarily from the United States. Naturally, we would be interested in something with a competitive return," Larry said.

Bobbi shifted in her chair and Manuel seemed to lose his train of thought. She couldn't help but smile just a little bit.

He recovered nicely and said, "You may well be a candidate for our 'Expression Account.' It is an aggressive market account that can be accessed from most of the world from any ATM machine. There is no service or maintenance charges whatsoever if a balance of $5000 U.S. is maintained. Withdrawals must be a minimum of $1000." He could tell from their expressions that the money would not be a problem. He continued, "I assure you that your account will be completely secure. Costa Rica boasts the most secure banks in the world. Some Caribbean countries might beg to differ but the figures do not lie. Your account will be 100 percent confidential. You can withdraw up to $10,000 from anywhere in the world, day or night, no questions asked. I'm sure you are aware that most ATM's won't give the average customer $10,000. Clients holding our 'expression' account have access to this and other privileges. Your own special four-digit access code will enable you to make this kind of withdrawal."

That was exactly what they wanted to hear. They filled out the paper work and deposited $10,000 into the account. Manuel shook Larry's hand and kissed Bobbi's. The light touch of his tongue on her wrist did not escape her. She smiled at him as they left.

Their two remaining days in San Jose were tarnished by the reality of upcoming events. Bobbi was strangely looking forward to her upcoming fling with Marko. He had always struck her as a passionate and confident man. She found herself hungering for his touch.

Larry said very little. The plan could work but not without Bobbi's involvement. They would pick up the broken pieces of their marriage later.

They left San Jose for Freeport Wednesday morning. There they finished out their stay in the Bahamas and flew home Friday morning.

*　　*　　*　　*

Wednesday morning found Jake pulling into the Hanslow Plantation. Gina Lacky was talking to Herndon Jones as Jake stepped out of his old truck. Gina smiled and Herndon stepped over to Jake's truck and looked it over.

"I take it spiritual advising doesn't pay real well," he said, noticing the big dent on Jake's passenger side.

"Herndon," Jake acknowledged, stepping out of the truck and putting on his robe. "How are you this fine day?"

"Blessed as usual. I'm sure you understand," Herndon said.

"Right," Jake muttered. "My dear," he said as Gina wandered over. Her long brown hair was flowing down her back complementing her model figure and perfect facial features.

"Salloa," she smiled. "Are the gods happy today?"

"I believe they are," he said. "Is Mona around?" Jake asked Gina.

"She is. Follow me, Swami," she said as she wiggled toward the front door with Jake right behind her.

As Mona entered the room Jake rose from his seat, bowed down, and kissed her hand.

"Lovely as usual," he said.

"Salloa," Mona said as Gina left the room. Glancing her way Mona said, "She's a lovely young lady. I'm sure you've noticed."

"This house has an abundance of beautiful women," Jake correctly said. She appreciated the compliment.

"What do we have this week?" she asked.

"He took a red head to the condo Monday evening from eight till ten. She had been there before. Late thirties, I don't think she's a dancer. She arrived in her own car, a black Lexus.

"My dear friend Carlotta, that whore. Marko's been screwing her for years," Mona said, drawing on her cigarette. "I take it you have film?" she asked as she crammed the cigarette butt viciously into an ashtray.

"Sure do, great shots on the camcorder, closeups. You want to see it?"

"Spare me," she said. "And tomorrow night?" she asked.

"I'll be there as usual," he said. "I wish I could get some inside shots."

"Well that isn't going to happen. I don't have a key. Do you think you could sneak in?"

"Not too likely," Jake said. "The windows are one piece, no way to open them. There's a deadbolt on the door." Jake shifted in his chair. "We are building quite a case against him. How much more do you think we need?"

"Are you getting tired?

"No. Just wondering."

"It'll be several more months. I want him by the balls."

You'll have to stand in line for that request, Jake thought.

They chatted a few more minutes and Jake wandered around for another hour or so before calling it a day.

* * * *

Sunday night, the twenty-seventh of November, the Grounds Barn crew arrived at the Hanslow Plantation at 7 P.M. Sam and Marie Conner arrived first followed by Larry and Bobbi Holder. Ted Miller came a few minutes later. The men were dressed in slacks and sport coats. The women wore long dresses. Bobbi's was split especially high up one side.

They were led to the dinning room where Gina served them roast duck and an assortment of superb vegetables. They were served an after-dinner wine in the study.

In nine years, they could count on one hand the number of times they had been invited to the plantation out of the blue. The annual Christmas party and a summertime pig picking were the usual extent of socializing with the Paskos. Though close to Christmas, this gathering did not represent that event. Something was up. They sipped their drinks and waited for Marko to speak. They didn't wait long.

"I appreciate your coming. We have had a number of good years together. Mona and I appreciate your loyalty and the good job you have done." All eyes were fixed on him as he continued. "Mona and I again wish to express our deep sorrow concerning the untimely deaths of your co-workers and friends," he spoke with trumped-up compassion that did not resonate with his audience. "Be that as it may, life must go on.... We are looking into the very real possibility of expanding our operation as it now stands." He took a drink of wine and continued. "Things in Columbia have taken a turn for the better as far as our operations go. A man whom we have relied heavily upon over the past several years has been elected as the head of police in the valley from which we get the majority of our marijuana. As a result, we will be able to have access to a better quality product and more of it. Our friends at Malpass Trucking are strongly encouraging us to double the size of our monthly shipment from the current level of five tons to ten tons. In addition, because of the quality of the new grass, our profits will more than double."

The group sat in rapt attention. The trap they found themselves in was getting deeper by the minute.

Mona rose and poured wine for all the guests and sat down.

Marko continued, "I understand and appreciate the risks that you have taken and continue to take. I have always felt that we have more than adequately compensated you for the risks involved; however, in light of this new development, it would only be right to compensate you in an appropriate manner. Effective the first of next year your salaries will be doubled."

With that announcement the group let out a collective gasp. They would each go from $60,000 to $120,000 per year. This meant the couples would be bringing in almost a quarter million annually! The wheels were turning in every head in the room.

"Mr. Holder, do you see any problem with doubling the capacity of the marijuana in the barn?" Marko realized that Larry was the intellectual of the group - a quiet man who thought before he spoke. His reflective way served him well as the spokesman for the group.

"The problem is not in the barn," Larry said. "The problem as I see it is that the security of the trucks will be compromised. Five tons is a whole lot easier to hide than ten tons." Larry drank the rest of his wine and stared at Marko with cold calculating eyes. Larry, unlike the others, was not intimidated by Marko and they both knew it.

"Very true, Mr. Holder," Marko said. "That very thing has crossed my mind as well. We are making appropriate arrangements in Columbia as far as the packaging goes. The new bags of grass will look like grass seed. It will look exactly like our winter rye grass bags, same markings, everything. If the trucks are searched they will see grass seed."

"What about dogs?" Larry said, looking up from his glass.

"Dogs are always a problem. They have not been a problem for nine years and I don't anticipate it happening now."

Mona rose and refilled the glasses again.

"Does anyone have anything else to say?" Marko asked not that any of them had a choice. He looked around the room at the faces. No outward hostility was noted. When his eyes met Bobbi's they lingered for a brief moment. His trained senses captured the unmistakable "come on" look of a willing woman. She turned slightly in her chair drawing attention to her long lean legs that Marko had admired for so long. A slight smile came to his face as the moment passed.

Mona added, "Marko has spoken of our concern for your safety and well being. I can assure you that I share his concern. We will not jeopardize your position just as I'm quite sure you would not ours. I am in full agreement concerning the new financial arrangements. It was one we did not have to make. We felt it was the right thing to do. I hope you appreciate that fact." Her words fell to a silent audience. Her astute comments left no doubt she was up to speed on every aspect of the operation. She could take over at a moment's notice and the operation would not miss a beat.

By nine o'clock, the guests were heading for the door. The men shook hands and the women hugged Marko. Bobbi lingered close to Marko as they embraced at the door. He whispered in her ear, "I'll be at the townhouse tomorrow at seven. Can you be there?"

Her slight nod was the only answer he needed. Only Larry noticed the exchange.

Chapter 8

JAKE ARRIVED AT THE THIRD AVENUE PIER at ten o'clock Monday morning. Joe Lane was seated at the counter sharing a cup of coffee with the pier owner, Ralph Causey. Joe usually referred to Ralph as "Bimbo."

"Gentlemen," Jake said, walking up and grabbing a stool. "Coffee, please," he said to Ralph.

"Sally gonna let you fish now? How nice." Joe said in his usual sarcastic nature. Jake ignored him. With Joe that was usually the best policy.

Jake sipped his coffee a moment or two. "Anything hitting out there?"   "Not really," Ralph said. "Been slow now for about three weeks. Most likely, it won't get any better for a while either. I am kind of surprised the trout aren't hitting."

"So how's Jane?" Jake asked Joe, figuring he would go ahead and risk a conversation with the old fart.

"Fine as usual. My women are always very content. You wouldn't know much about that."

"You might be surprised," Jake said.

"You playing any golf?" Ralph asked, seeing the conversation needed help.

"Yeah, sure have. I've been playing up at Droughbrigh. You ever been out there?"

"I've played there a time or two. It's been a while. The place is too rich for me. How can you afford that place?" Ralph asked.

"It's called a free pass. What can I say?"

"You must be living right," Ralph said. "Does your client own it?"

"Like, I'm going to tell you," Jake said.

"Why anybody with money would hire you is a mystery to me," Joe said.

"Funny how that works," Jake said. "I guess I'm so damned charming these women just can't resist me."

"Give me some cut bait, Bimbo. Fishing's got to be better than this," Joe said handing Ralph a couple of bucks. "Take your time," he said to Jake as he grabbed his pole and walked toward the pier.

"You got strange taste in friends," Ralph said as he poured Jake another cup of coffee.

*   *   *   *

Bobbi Holder pulled out from her driveway for the ten-minute drive to Marko's townhouse. She had never been there but everyone at the Barn knew where it was and what it was there for. The day had been a cold one between her and Larry. They hadn't spoken ten words all day. He smoked one joint after another. She did not. She needed to be at her best. She had to make this visit worth an invite back from Marko. Marko was in for quite a treat!

As usual Jake had arrived at the complex at six-thirty and had set up his equipment. Marko had not failed to show up yet.

Marko arrived a few minutes before Bobbi. He poured a drink and waited. He heard a slight tap on the door. He opened it to find her there.

"Come in," he said as she stepped through the door. He took her jacket. "Would you care for a drink?"

"Rum and Coke," she said. Marko's confident manner had always been a turn on for her. Tonight, her passions would be released.

He handed her a drink and sat in a chair directly across from her. She sipped her drink and put it down. She rose and walked over to Marko and placed her body between his legs and kissed him with a hot wet kiss.

Marko had never had a woman give herself to him so freely and with such animalistic hunger. The dancers he bought and paid for were so mechanical. Bobbi's passion and desire were at a fever pitch. Looking for the password was not on her mind.

Two hours of passionate play had left them both exhausted. She picked up her coat and prepared to leave.

"When can you return?" he asked.

"Whenever you want me, Marko."

"How could I not want you? Can you be here Thursday at the same time?"

She kissed him again and said, "You know I will. I'm just warming up."

"That's hard to believe," he said. "What does Larry think of you going out?"

"Piss on Larry," she said. She kissed him again. "I'll see you Thursday," she said, heading out the door and closing it as she left.

Marko poured himself another drink and sat back in his chair. *This certainly complicates things,* he thought as he remembered the evening.

Jake recorded her leaving and packed up his stuff and headed home.

*　　*　　*　　*

"A massage is so relaxing, don't you think?" Monty asked as his fingers worked the deep muscles in Mona's bare shoulder. "You are so exquisite," he said, admiring her nude from the waist up figure lying face down on the table. "And what is Marko up to these days?"

"Screwing everything in sight, what else," she said. "I'm more selective," she said, smiling his way. "He's going out of the country for ten days starting Saturday. I'm going to Cancun for the week. Company wouldn't be bad," she said, looking over her shoulder at Monty with inviting eyes.

"If that's an offer, I'm flattered, but I'm afraid I can't. I might have told you awhile back that I was engaged. She's coming to town and I need to be here. Any other time and it would have been great."

"Can't blame a girl for trying," she said.

"Don't stop trying, darling. It might just happen.... I'm sure you'll find someone to talk to," he said with a smile.

"No doubt," Mona had to agree. She had more in mind than talking.

*   *   *   *

"So, you don't see a problem?" Marko asked Harone as they sat at a window table in a small Italian restaurant in the Market district of Charleston. It was six o'clock Tuesday evening.

"No problem," he said, waving his hand. "The dock foreman's in my pocket. He wouldn't fart without my ok."

"Twice as much weed... manpower won't be a problem?"

Harone grabbed his brother's chin. "Read my lips...it's no problem, my brother.... So, are you going to Columbia soon?"

"Yes. I want to congratulate Ellias on being elected." Marko took a big swig of his draft. "Deputy of Police, can you believe it?"

"Quite amazing indeed. Is Mona going with you?" Harone was always interested in Mona.

"She'll be staying.... She may go on a trip somewhere. She usually does.... I don't know."

"Are you going alone?"

"I don't think so. I've found a suitable traveling companion.... Yes, she's quite acceptable," he said, smiling as their spaghetti arrived.

"Do I know her?" Harone asked.

Marko looked up from his plate, "Bobbi... Bobbi Holder."

"Oh, my.... You are a lucky man. And her husband?"

"She says, 'piss on him.'"

"Does Mona know?"

"No. She doesn't need to know about my women. I take care of her very well. I'm sure Brenda knows very little of your escapades."

"And I hope to keep it that way. Have you asked Bobbi to go yet?"

"Not yet. She will say yes. She's incredibly hot for me. I've never had another woman like her." Marko stared out the window. "She will go with me. You can be sure of that."

They finished their meal and Marko was on his way.

*　　*　　*　　*

"Now, let me get this... you say that God is in everything... Is that right?" Herndon asked Salloa bright and early Wednesday morning.

Herndon Jones was a likable guy and under normal circumstances, he would be great company. But dealing with a spiritually astute person didn't make Jake's cover as a "new age" spiritual guide any easier to pull off. It did make their encounters quite challenging. Jake wished he would just talk about the weather or something like that. It would make life so much easier.

"That's right, Mr. Jones, God is manifested in everything."

"So God is in that horse turd over there," he said, scratching his chin. "This is really amazing stuff. I never would have dreamed it."

"I think it's a bit blasphemous to refer to God as a horse turd," Salloa countered.

"That's my feeling exactly. I was just taking your argument to its logical conclusion. If God is in everything, then He's in that horse turd. That is what you're saying, isn't it?"

"God is in the horse turd but He is not a horse turd," Salloa, said. He could see that he was losing ground here. "The essence of God is in everything."

"Oh, the essence of God. I wondered what that smell was. Tell me, is God male or female?" Herndon asked.

This guy loves pulling my chain, Jake thought. He said, "God is beyond sexuality as we know it. He is 'one' with both men and women." *That sounded good,* Jake thought.

"So God, as you see Him, does not place women in a place of submission to men," Herndon stated.

"That is correct. How could a good god do that?" the great Salloa asked. "The divine families of men and women are completely equal."

"What happens if a very hard decision needs to be made and it needs to be made now? Who takes the responsibility for making that decision?"

In desperation, the "Great One" looked around and saw a bikini clad Gina heading around back of the big house to sunbathe. He did appreciate these eighty-degree November days. "They will just know. The Divine will bear witness to their collective spirit.... I really need to move on, Herndon. We will chat again soon," Salloa said as he made a beeline for the young woman who happened to be carrying a cooler of beer. His robe flapped like a super-hero and the sun glared from his bald head as he shot toward the back yard.

"Jake! What the hell are you doing?" Mona snapped as she spotted Salloa hustling after the young woman.

"Oh, ah ... Mona. How are you this fine morning?"

"I'm fine, Salloa, but you look like a complete fool. Don't tell me... You were going to anoint her with oil?"

Damn, I didn't bring any with me, Jake thought. "No. I just wanted to chat. I hadn't spoken to her recently."

"Aren't you the considerate one? Step in here for a minute if you can take a moment from your busy schedule."

Jake followed her into the house. Mona was obviously a little edgy today. It might be the time of the month.

"Has our boy been misbehaving?" she asked as they took a seat in the den.

"Yep. He was with another girl last night. Same scenario, they were there a couple of hours and she left. She came in her own car. I don't know if she was a dancer. She could have been. She drove a Mazda."

"What did she look like?" Mona asked.

"Tall, leggy brunette, short hair, fairly attractive, definitely sensual. Do you want to see the film?"

"Not right now. I'm sure she's good looking. Marko does have his standards," she said, putting out her cigarette. "Marko will be leaving the country for a week to ten days December first. I won't need you during that time. Will twenty dollars a day hold your services while he's away?" she asked.

Twenty dollars a day for doing nothing sounded good to Jake. "Sure, that sounds fine." He hoped this gravy train never ended.

"You won't need to come this Friday. Just do your usual filming of Marko's exploits at the townhouse. I will pay you for your work now. I think I can trust you," she said with squinting eyes. She counted out fifteen hundred dollars and handed him the money.

"I will be out of town myself. I will call you around the tenth."

"Are you traveling with Marko?" Jake asked.

"It's none of your damn business, and no, I'm not," she said.

She acted like she had things to do and Jake got up to leave.

"I guess I'll hang around a little while. I might talk to Gina a few minutes."

"Just try acting like a spiritual advisor, ok?"

"No problem," Jake smiled.

"And if I see you drinking beer you're fired...Do you understand?"

"Crystal clear...beautiful...no problem," he managed to utter as he backed to the door.

She gave him a "it better be" look and walked out of the room. The girl had quite a sway Jake noticed as she waltzed off. If Sally only knew what he had to put up with here.... He wasn't planning on telling her.

"Hey, Salloa," Gina said with a big smile as she looked over her sunglasses. "The cooler's full, have one."

"I'll have to be the designated observer today."

"Don't they teach you to hold your liquor in seminary or wherever the hell you went?" Her bikini the last time was blue. This one was yellow.

"I was out of line last time, my dear. I should have known better. Can I help you with that?" he said as she applied suntan lotion to her shoulders and legs.

"Tell you what, swami, I'll get this side and you can get my back side."

"My pleasure," he said as she turned over. And to think he was actually getting paid for this!

* * * *

Larry and Bobbi had not spoken since her Monday night visit. He had to assume she had not yet acquired the computer code information. She wasn't saying.

She left Thursday evening for her return rendezvous with Markos. She wore an extremely short black skirt with a white top. Jake filmed her as she arrived.

Marko ravished her as she stepped through the door. An hour later she rested in his arms in his king-size waterbed.

"I need you here tomorrow, same time.... Will there be a problem?"

"What do you think?" she said, exhaling a circle of cigarette smoke. "I'll be here...and you know it, too."

Marko smiled at his conquest, "I think you will."

"Smart boy," she said.

"There is something else," he said. "I leave Saturday for Bogota. I want you to go. We will be gone ten days." He waited for a response.

The feelings she had this week had gone way beyond what she had expected. She could not keep herself away from him now. She would go anywhere with him and do anything for him. She wanted him that much. Finding something to blackmail him with was not at the top of her current agenda.

"I would leave tonight if you wanted me to... What about Mona?"

"What about her?" he said, gazing at the ceiling. "What she doesn't know won't hurt her. I'll pick you up at your house at noon. Your husband will be at work. The crew can manage the Saturday work without you."

"What should I tell Larry?"

"Tell him I need your services."

She left shortly before ten and returned again Friday evening.

CHAPTER 9

J AKE'S LONG SIGH was a sure sign he was faced with
    something a little unpleasant. The present reason for
    anxiety was the Saturday morning dance class. Jake had
always suspected that he had two left feet. His closely held
secret was now becoming public knowledge.

"You're doing great," Sally told him as they drove toward
North Myrtle. Their destination was the Beach Dance School
and a rendezvous with their trusty and long-suffering instructor,
Bonnie Harpon. Bonnie was nice enough but just a little too
pushy to suit Jake. Pushy was a necessary trait for any good
dance instructor. Otherwise plenty of adequate dancers would
not have been "pushed" into it.

"Sally... Jake," Bonnie said as they walked in. On any given
Saturday twenty to twenty-five dancers would show up. When
Jake agreed to learn to shag he figured it would be easy enough
and it wouldn't hurt his love life. He had no idea that a simple
dance like the shag could have all these different variations.
Drill sergeant Harpon seemed to love putting Jake through the
paces. If it were not for Sally's insistence that they practice at
home, Jake would have given up some time earlier.

Thirty minutes into the lesson Bonnie gathered the dancers
together and awarded several small prizes including "Most
Improved Dancer" which she promptly awarded to Jake.

Though still one of the worse dancers there, compared to where he started he looked like Fred Astaire. Sally gave him a kiss on the cheek, which was followed by a round of applause.

Bonnie figured Jake needed some encouragement. It would be a little easier coming the next week.

*   *   *   *

Marko pulled into Bobbi's drive at five till twelve Saturday morning. She was out the door in two minutes with her luggage. They looked at each other with hungry eyes and were on their way.

At one thirty Saturday afternoon Mona took off for Cancun. She was not intending on behaving herself.

Marko and Bobbi arrived at the International El Dorado Airport just outside of Bogota shortly before 10 P.M. The city sprawled across the vast valley and was home to some six million people. They caught a cab to the modern section and checked into the DeLora Hotel in a sixteenth floor honeymoon suite.

A thousand miles away, Mona checked into the Maleen Hotel and Resort in Cancun.

*   *   *   *

The week that Bobbi left with Marko was the worst week of Larry's life. Their marriage had lost what little spark it had left. The nightmare of what was happening now was more than he could bear. He tried to hide the reality of his crumbling life from his co-workers at the Grounds Barn. It didn't work. He told them she went to see her mother. No one believed him. They had seen this trouble coming. They had no idea Bobbi was seeing Marko, but they all figured she had left him for another man.

It tore at Larry that she was with Marko. The fact that she was enjoying it so much was the worst part. He was enraged and yet helpless. It was after all, his idea. He drank himself to sleep Saturday night.

*　　*　　*　　*

"What ya think?" Jill Arthur asked. She was entering a dance contest sponsored by the local elementary school that her daughter attended. She was doing a little bump and wiggle that would have looked good with most any woman doing it. With her slim legs and tight black slacks, it was enough to make Jake want to forget his manners. "Really... What do you think?" she said again.

"Honey, I believe you can pick up your prize," he said.

"And what might that be?"

"Two glorious nights in a motel of your choice with yours truly."

"Wow, every woman's dream," she said.

"What can I say?"

"You're just too easy, Jake," she said as she poured him another cup of coffee and sat down across from him. "You still working up north of town?"

"Yep. It's been a good job. The lady pays real well."

"Spying on somebody's old man I'm sure."

"What can I say. It's a private eye's bread and butter."

"How much longer you gonna be working for her?"

"A few more months...I don't know for sure. I'm just taking it a week at a time. I've got a ten-day break right now. So if you want to drag me off to some exotic location now's your chance."

"I don't get off till five," she said with a wink.

"I can wait," Jake said.

Jill got up and smiled at Jake saying, "We're just full of it."

"I know, but it is fun," Jake said.

"That it is, Jake Brown...that it is," she said as she headed off to wait on a couple that just came in.

Jake finished his coffee and cruised out the door.

*   *   *   *

Marko and Bobbi spent Sunday and Monday sightseeing in Bogota. They visited a number of places, including the Gold Museum, the San Francisco Church, the National Cathedral, and the Shrine of the Monserrate.

Monday evening found them sitting on a bench watching the boat traffic on the Fucha River. Their whirlwind romance had been more than a mere affair, especially for Bobbi. She felt something had been born inside her that had long been dead. The gentle evening breeze felt good in their faces.

"These last couple of days have been great," Bobbi said. "It's been so long since my life has had any joy." She looked ahead and continued. "I wish I could stay here forever."

Marko didn't say anything. He wished she could, too. Leave the complications of Myrtle Beach behind. Bobbi would be a welcome reason for any trip to Columbia. He would not consider staying in Columbia himself. There was too much going on in the states - business, the women, and beautiful, alluring, Mona.

"Your staying here is not out of the question. I could work it out," he said. "I'm sure I could find an excuse to see you four or five times a year. Mona would never find out, not that she cares what I do," he said with just a twinge of regret. "Larry, now there is another matter. He certainly complicates things."

Yes, he does, she thought. The joy that they had once known was now a distant memory. Their life together had gone from excitement and desire to resignation and routine. She did love him. That was an amazing thing in itself. She loved him and yet she was willing to walk out of his life and never see him again. There would be no tears on her part. She had cried herself to sleep too many times.

They sat and stared across the river. Boats of every description came by. Most were work boats of one fashion or another - so unlike the affluent river scenes that were scattered throughout the United States.

"I could set you up with a place here," Marko said, looking across the river as Bobbi looked intently at his rugged profile. "You could be our local liaison here. It would be good for business to have you here. If you come back to the states it's only a matter of time that Mona would find out about you. That would not be good.... It's not like you're one of the whores that I've been hanging around with."

"It's not?" she said, hoping that she meant more than that to him. "If I've been your whore, then I hope it never ends," she said as tears formed in her eyes. She wondered if she was falling in love with this brutal man. Whatever her feelings were, she had no intention of stopping them. "I want to stay here, Marko. I want my life to change and I want it to include you, even if it means only seeing you every few months. I don't want to give up what we have." She leaned into him and gently kissed his lips. "Set it up for me, Marko. I want to stay here."

*   *   *   *

Tuesday morning Marko and Bobbi drove their rented a car for the three hour drive to Chapinero to see Marko's business acquaintance, Ellias Manuel, the newly elected Deputy of Police of the Keora Valley. The district included the most productive marijuana and cocaine production in the world. Major drug money support was a prerequisite for being elected to any office in Columbia. Mr. Manuel had plenty of drug money behind him.

Marko and Bobbi arrived at his home shortly before noon and were met at the gate by two men carrying rifles. They stopped the car as it approached the gate.

"Mr. Pasko to see Mr. Manuel," Marko said to the stern looking guard. The guard stepped to the guardhouse and made a phone call. He waited a moment and walked back to the car.

"He's expecting you," the guard said in broken English as he looked in the window and across at Bobbi. "Straight ahead," he said.

Marko pulled through the gate. The Manuel estate was rather plain by U.S. standards but impressive nonetheless. Summer flowers were in bloom and the sky was full of exotic birds. A three-acre lake ran next to the drive and was filled with aquatic life. A servant opened the car door as they came to a stop. They were led into the house and were met there by Ellias Manuel.

Bobbi was struck by Ellias Manuel's appearance. He was the most handsome man she had ever seen - a very cultured man who spoke perfect English. She had not expected a man so heavily influenced by drug money to command such a presence. There was much she would learn during her stay in Columbia.

"Marko," the gracious and confident man said. "My pleasure as always... and this is?" he asked, smiling toward Bobbi.

"Bobbi Holder... Ellias Manuel," Marko said.

"A beautiful woman is always welcome here," he graciously said as he kissed her hand.

"Thank you," she returned.

For the next hour, he showed Bobbi and Marko around his block home which was filled with priceless works of art and beautiful furniture.

After lunch, they relaxed in Ellias's smoking room where he and Marko enjoyed a fine cigar. Bobbi sipped on a glass of fine sherry.

"When will you begin your official duties as Deputy of Police?" Marko asked.

Manuel laughed. "My friend, in Columbia you take over your duties the minute you are declared the winner. This is not the United States. We are much more civilized here."

He might be right, Bobbi thought. *That was scary with Columbia being the drug capital of the world.*

"And you will be staying in our fair country for a while... how nice," Ellias said addressing Bobbi. "Of course, you are welcome to stay here."

"I'm sure you would like that my friend," Marko said. "I need to separate her from smooth talking men. She is so vulnerable... you do understand."

"Columbia is not the country for her then. Besides, she doesn't strike me as vulnerable, anything but," he said with admiring eyes.

"Two handsome, successful men, carrying on over me. I must be doing something right," Bobbi said.

"You are doing much right, my darling," Marko said. "I have obtained a place for her in town overlooking the river. It will be quite adequate for her."

"Well, I had to offer," Ellias Manuel said.

"Have you talked to Theo?" Marko asked.

"Mr. Marianno. Yes, I have. He is doing well. He speaks highly of you and your operation."

"He discussed with you his proposal?"

"Yes. We talked at length."

"Do you see a problem?"

"There are no problems, my friend, only challenges. It will be a small thing to do."

"And the quality?"

"The quality? When has quality ever been a problem?"

"There has not been a problem but we are doubling the cargo. Mr. Marianno will not be compromised."

Ellias took a long drag on his cigar and smiled again at Bobbi. "Mr. Marianno will not be disappointed.... I tell you the truth, Marko. Men like Marianno are bought and sold in Columbia every day. He does not concern me and he certainly doesn't frighten me. Be that as it may, the product will be excellent as usual."

"And the shippers?" Marko asked.

"The shippers...? Have you seen the port near Barranguilla, Marko?"

"No, we plan to visit Thursday," Marko said.

"When you go you will be amazed at how busy it is. I mean ships lined up to get into that place. Bags of coffee everywhere you look. Most of the bags don't have coffee in them and everybody knows it. I mean everybody: Marko, the police, the military, the churches, the unions - everybody knows it. There's no need to worry about the shippers. This is what they do. They traffic in drugs... period. A dissenter would be dead in a week. This world is not big enough to hide in. It would be suicide. You're in Columbia, my friend. We are very efficient when it comes to drugs."

"Is it taken from here in trucks?" Marko asked.

"It is trucked to the river."

"And the river flows into Barranquilla?" Marko asked.

"Yes, the Magdalena River, the pride of Columbia. It's a beautiful place, my dear. I must take you some time," he said, looking at Bobbi.

She looked at Marko who shrugged his approval. With that she said, "I'm looking forward to it." *Columbia is looking better all the time,* she thought.

"Will the double shipment be in place by the first of the year?" Marko asked.

"Again, there will not be a problem. Your tonnage is nothing more than a drop in the bucket of what this valley produces. We keep the world in drugs, Marko, not just Baltimore," he laughed.

At this Ellias arose and took Bobbi by the hand and led them for a tour of his flowering gardens. As dusk approached, Marko and Bobbi said goodbye and drove back to Bogota.

CHAPTER 10

LARRY HOLDER ARRIVED at the Grounds Barn at seven-thirty Tuesday morning. His head was splitting from the heavy drinking of the night before. Ted, Sam, and Marie Conner were gathered around the table drinking coffee and reading the paper when Larry walked in. They all saw the problems coming with Larry and Bobbi's marriage. They didn't blame either one of them. It was one of those marriages where everything was just too much of a struggle. Beneath all the crap they endured, there was a hint of something sweet. It just didn't surface often enough to salvage what they had left.

"Larry," Marie said, grabbling Larry's arm as they stood together at the coffeepot. "You all right?" she asked. Being a "mother hen" was as natural to her as breathing.

He shrugged his shoulders and said, "I'm just hanging on. I keep thinking that tomorrow will be better. It hasn't happened yet." He grabbed her elbow and looked into her sincere eyes and said, "Thanks for asking."

He sat down at the table and Ted Miller promptly gave him a mild slug on the shoulder and said, "Hombre," which was Ted's way of saying, "I'm right here, pal."

"Blood," Larry said to Ted. Looking across the table at Sam Conner he said, "Morning."

Sam nodded acknowledgement and everybody went back to their coffee, crosswords, and puzzles. Several minutes passed without any comment. Marie finally broke the ice.

"We're all here for you, Larry. We just want you to know that. We've been through too much together. You can count on us."

"I can count on you.... I don't know about those two," he said, waving toward the men.

"Can you believe he said that?" Sam asked Ted.

"It's hard to believe. I'm crushed," Ted said.

"Any idea where she is?" Marie asked.

He had no idea except she was somewhere with Marko. That fact he would keep to himself. No point in adding insult to injury. The reality was that it was his damn idea and it was eating him alive. The way she reacted to the fling with Marko was something he had not expected.

He shrugged his shoulders and said, "I don't know where she is. She could be on the moon for all I know."

"You gonna take her back if she shows up?" Ted asked.

"I don't know."

They chatted a few more minutes and went about the day's work. Larry had never been so grateful for his friends at the Barn. He was prone to keep everything inside. They were not going to let that happen.

*   *   *   *

The drive to Barranquilla was an all-day affair from Bogota. The roads were rough and rarely allowed traffic to navigate over fifty miles per hour. The drive was both beautiful and frightening. Every turn in the road presented the possibility that they could be robbed. Fifty miles outside of Barranquilla, the road began to run along the Magdalena River. Ellias's description of the river as the "Pride of Columbia" was not an exaggeration. The clear blue-green river flowed peacefully toward the sea. It was hard to believe that this picturesque river carried a full quarter of the world's drugs.

Barranguilla, six miles upstream from the Atlantic Ocean, was a bustling port city of 700,000 inhabitants. The large mouth of the river was the ideal harbor for the merchant ships as they awaited their precious cargo.

Marko and Bobbi obtained a hotel suite in the downtown area. The room was spacious with a beautiful fifth floor view of the town-square. Businessmen, street vendors, and hookers filled the dirty streets.

"This is so exciting. I love this life," Bobbi said half to herself while looking out the window. Marko came and put his arms around her waist. His touch took her breath away. "Maybe, I love you too," she softly said as tears formed in her eyes. She turned toward him and they fell together on the king size bed.

The next morning, following a robust breakfast, they caught a cab to the shipping area and to the office of La Capa Shipping. The building was a small framed building that sat on the road two hundred yards from the river. Similar operations were the norm.

Ellias Manuel was accurate in that the shipyard was a very busy place. The placard on the door simply read, "La Capa." Marko and Bobbi stepped into the small paper-cluttered office. Several girlie calendars from years gone by adorned the walls. The air was filled with the smell of old food, cigar smoke, and God knows what else.

Honanne Bues sat behind the desk. Fifty and a little overweight, he was chewing on a cheap cigar and looking over some crumbled papers. He looked up when Marko and Bobbi walked in. "Yes," he said, revealing several gaps where his teeth used to be.

"Marko Pasko," Marko said, extending his hand, "This is my special friend and business associate, Bobbi. We're from the States, South Carolina."

"Yes, Mr. Pasko. I spoke to your brother Harone yesterday evening. He said you might stop by," Mr. Bues stated. "Welcome to Barranquilla. I admire a man who can mix business with pleasure," he said, glancing at Bobbi. "I assume this is business?"

"A little of both, my friend," Marko answered.

"Well... La Capa welcomes you."

"Quite a bustling town you have here," Marko said.

"I've lived here all my life," Honanne said in surprisingly clear if not distinguished English. "Are you enjoying our fair-city, senorita?"

"Yes, I love it. It is so different than what I'm used to," she said. "The people seem so nice."

I imagine everybody's nice to you, Honanne Bues thought. "Yes. We're a very social people," he said. "Would you like some coffee? It's the best in the world."

They drank a cup of excellent coffee and engaged in several minutes of idle chat. A few customers and workers came in and out. When they were alone they got back to business.

"So what brings you here? I know you have not come all the way to Barranquilla to drink my coffee," Honanne Bues rightly observed.

Marko wiped his lips and said, "Your excellent reputation precedes you. We have heard nothing but good things concerning your operation."

"Our good name is only as good as our last job," Honanne said.

Marko continued, "I'm sure you know that we have been importing product from Columbia for a number of years. We have had continuous business with your fine country for nine years. We hope to have many more years of mutual prosperity."

"Of course," Mr. Bues said.

"We are strongly considering doubling our freight each month. We have made arrangements with the producers and we need to be sure that this can be handled from your end," Marko said as he waited for an answer.

"I can assure you, Mr. Pasko, there will be no problem. The nature of your cargo demands special treatment. We have more than enough workers and ships to handle much larger jobs than what you're talking about."

"Excellent," Marko said. "Any problems with the local authorities?"

"You mean the police?" Honanne asked.

"Yes."

Honanne smiled, "The police are no problem in Barranquilla. This is what we do here. The police are really our allies. They sometimes put on a show for the international authorities, but I can assure you it is nothing to worry about. The police are in our pocket. They are really our best friends. Who would they report a problem to, the newspaper? That's a joke. The newspapers, the radio, the TV, they are all owned by the drug lords. You see, my friend, we are all in this together. It is what we do here, not to worry," he said wagging his hairy finger at Marko.

The three of them strolled to the dock area and watched as the men worked freight onto a mid-sized La Capa liner. Pallet after pallet of coffee and spice bags were loaded onto the rusty boat. The operation looked efficient. After observing the operation Marko felt confident they could do the job.

"I will be heading back to the states in a few days. If I need to talk, I will send word by Bobbi. She will be staying on in Columbia."

That news got Honanne's attention.

"She has your number. She will be checking in from time to time," Marko said.

"Excellent," Honanne said. "I'm looking forward to our new working arrangement. I'm sure it will be profitable for all of us."

They bid farewell and made the drive back to Bogota.

I couldn't be so lucky, Honanne thought as he watched Bobbi walk away.

*   *   *   *

"I'm retired, Jake. I don't need a job. I especially don't need one working for you," Rudy Rogers said as he and Jake enjoyed coffee and biscuit at the Beach Deli. The day had begun with eighteen holes of golf at Droughbrigh Country Club - their weekly round of free golf.

"I ain't talking about right now. I don't need you now," Jake said, waving his hand in the air. "Sometime, I might need you. That's all I'm saying."

"What's good for stress?" Jill Arthur asked as she leaned over the table where they were sitting. "I'm tight as a drum."

"I've got a relaxing technique that would just drive you up the wall," Rudy said. "You need to come over to my place and let me demonstrate it."

"Is that the only thing you learned at the police department?" she asked, throwing Jake a wink. "Besides, Jake might get mad and just have to slap you."

"That's right," Jake said. "You see these hands?" he said holding them up. "These babies are registered with the State of

South Carolina. Look no further, darling. Your answer is sitting right here."

"Right under my nose, too," she said. "It just goes to show you."

She walked across the floor to give a customer a refill. They were mesmerized by her sway as she crossed the room.

"Could you stand being twenty years younger?" Rudy asked.

"I can remember twenty years ago and twenty years ago didn't look that good, no time no where," Jake said.

"When you going back to work?" Rudy asked changing the subject.

"Next week, I guess. They're out of town this week."

"Where did they go?"

"I don't know. All I know is they went different directions."

"Money will do that," Rudy said. They finished their coffee and went their ways.

*   *   *   *

The week flew by for Marko and Bobbi. They busied themselves furnishing her apartment overlooking the Fucha River. Good furniture was expensive but they did manage to find some deals.

Bobbi's new name was Bobbi Thimpkin. Thanks to Ellias Manuel, she had a complete set of I.D.'s including a passport.

Marko left for home on Sunday afternoon with a promise to call every week. He planned a return visit in February. Marko arrived in Myrtle Beach late Sunday evening. Mona got in the day before.

Bobbi settled into her new life as Ms. Bobbi Thimpkin. She was really enjoying her new freedom. She wondered how Larry was making it. She knew it was hard for him but she was confident he would survive. It puzzled her why she thought of him as often as she did.

She wasn't suffering much. The men in Columbia were drawn to their new visitor. She enjoyed the attention but had no intention of being unfaithful to Marko, not that she thought he was saving himself for her.

*   *   *   *

Monday evening after Marko's return, Jake went back to work gathering dirt. To Jake's surprise Marko didn't bring a woman to his Dortshire townhouse. Marko showed up at seven and left at nine. *First time for everything,* Jake thought.

Tuesday morning found Salloa back at the Hanslow Plantation. Billy Pasko was out of school for the day. The one constant about Billy was you could be sure he was up to no good.

Jake checked in with Mona and relayed to her that Marko had been a good boy the night before. She seemed disappointed and was sure that it would only be a momentary lapse. *He must have worn himself out in Columbia,* she thought.

Jake spent some time wandering through the large house. He said a couple of words to Marko who ignored him.

Walking though the upstairs hall he heard a scuffling sound overhead and noticed the door leading to the attic was ajar. He quietly pulled down the attic steps and climbed up.

The attic was dark except for a little light let in by a ridge vent. Several attic fans were humming along as fans often do in the South. The attic was well boarded and tall enough to stand up in. Every few steps Jake stopped and listened. Something more than the fans was stirring up there.

Jake walked across the front of the house and turned the corner to ease down the back wing when he saw the silhouette of a figure lying on the floor. Jake slowly approached until he was no more than ten feet from the figure. It was Billy. He seemed to be looking at something below. A nearby fan running made Jake's approach undetected. He knelt next to Billy and watched him a moment or two. Whatever Billy was watching, he seemed to be enjoying it, if his gyrations meant anything.

Jake leaned over next to Billy's ear and said, "Can I look?"

Jake startled the poor boy so that he almost 1 jumped out of his skin. He sat up quickly and managed to put his hand over the hole he was looking through.

"You ok, Billy?"

"I'm fine, damn it. What the hell are you doing up here?"

"I could ask you the same thing.... Actually, I heard a noise and I thought it might have been a burglar or something. I was relieved to see it was only you.... What were you looking at?"

"I wasn't looking at anything," he said not very loud and with his hand obviously covering something up.

"Are you covering up a hole in the floor, Billy? You aren't peeping at someone are you?"

"Bite me, Swami. It ain't none of your damn business what I'm doing. I don't need to answer to a flunky like you."

There was nothing Jake hated worse than a fifteen-year old, fat, smart- ass.

"I'm afraid I'm going to have to take a look, Billy," Jake said as he wrestled Billy's hand away from the hole. Jake stooped down and took a look. The hole had been drilled directly above the bathtub of Gina Lacky who happened to be sprawled out in the tub directly below.... Jake briefly thought he had died and gone to heaven.... Being indignant would have been the "appropriate" response. He was going to have to fake it.

Getting up he looked at the boy and said, "Billy, you should know better than this. She would kill you if she found out."

"She ain't going to find out, clown.... Do you understand?"

God, I'd like to slap this kid, Jake thought. He was one of those punks who would make it hard to keep the smile off your face as you beat him about the head and shoulders. "You don't think I should tell Gina that she is being violated?" Jake finally managed.

"I ain't violating the bitch. I'm just enjoying the view," the little nerd said.

"How would you like her spying on you?" Jake asked.

"I couldn't be so lucky," Billy said.

Jake could relate to that. It did bother him a little that he thought somewhat along the same lines as this little twerp.

"I have half a mind to tell your mother about this," Jake said.

"I doubt if you'd do that, swami. This cabbage is just a little too green."

"What are you talking about?"

"Oh, nothing, except I saw the great Salloa drinking beer and flirting with Ginger out at the Club. You didn't even have your swami outfit on. I have a feeling that you aren't what you say you are and I don't think you would want this gravy to come to an end. I don't know what dear old Momma is paying you but I can imagine it's more than you're used to. Like I said, the cabbage is a little too green around here to screw with me. Daddy just might find out a thing or two about Salloa."

Jake could feel the perspiration forming on his brow. This little scumbag was quite the wheeler-dealer. He was right about one thing, Jake didn't want this ride to end - between the money and free golf. A few choice words would put him on Marko's list real quick and Jake didn't like the thought of that.

"You leave me alone and I leave you alone. Got it?"

Jake couldn't believe he was working out a deal with this brat. The kid had his number and he had no choice but to give in.

"I guess we got a deal, cowboy," Jake said.

"Well, get the hell out of here then," he said, waving Jake away. "She's gonna be in there a while," he said resuming his position.

Jake shook his head and walked away leaving the boy to his own sick devices.

CHAPTER 11

ITT WAS NOT SOMETHING HE LOOKED FORWARD TO but it needed to be done. Marko dialed the number. "Larry, this is Marko. I need to see you Friday for lunch. We need to talk. Take the day off work. Meet me at the Delray Café on sixteenth at 11:30. See you then."

Larry Holder played the message on his recorder a second time. Larry's emotions ran between rage and relief at the thought of confronting Marko. Rage that Marko had pursued and caught his wife, relief that it was coming to a head. He pulled the tab on a beer and sat in his easy chair and stewed. *Two days to wait and not enough beer in Myrtle Beach,* Larry thought. This was one appointment he would not miss.

*   *   *   *

The Thursday night stakeout at the townhouse had a bit of a twist this time. Marko changed things up by bringing in two girls, a blond and a redhead. Three hours later they emerged. So much for Marko's new leaf.

*   *   *   *

114

Larry arrived at the Delray Café at exactly 11:30 Friday morning. Marko was sitting at a corner table and waved Larry over. Larry eased into the seat across from him. The cold chill in the stares between the two men was apparent.

"She pursued me. I did what any man would do. She's a beautiful woman. I'm sorry." Marko had wanted her for years but in this case it was true enough. She had pursued him.

Larry lit a cigarette and continued his icy stare at Marko. He was not in the social mood.

Marko continued, "I am not seeing her now. In fact, she has left the area. She said she needed a change in her life. So she left. I don't know where."

Larry continued his chilling stare. He didn't believe him.

"She wanted me to tell you that she was sorry but she had to go on with her life."

"It's a sorry damn world," Larry finally said.

"At times, it is," Marko said. "But we must go on with life."

"She was my life. Two people committed to one another. You've heard of that concept, haven't you?" Larry seethed. "Damn empty without her. Know what I mean? Don't much give a damn right now. Live or die, I don't care."

They placed their lunch order and Marko said, "What am I going to do with you, Larry? Can a man in my position afford an employee who is ready to kill himself?"

"I would like to keep you on. You've been nothing but an asset for me. I made a mistake. Everybody makes mistakes. What am I going to do with you? How can I keep someone around who is ready to end it all?"

Larry stirred his coffee and looked across the table at Marko. "I didn't say I wanted to quit or kill myself. My co-workers are the only friends I got. They keep me going."

"Can I count on you, Larry? That's what I need to know."

"You can count on me. I ain't going nowhere."

"Good," Marko said.

"Something else," Larry said, "don't give me that crap that you didn't pursue her. You have been after her as long as I've known you. We both know that."

"Fair enough," he said.

They ate their lunch in silence. Drinking a final cup of coffee, Marko said, "You know I couldn't let you just walk away. Like it or not, if you plan on seeing tomorrow you will work at Droughbrigh." Marko looked at him with cold condescending eyes. "I'm sure you figured that one out. Didn't you, Larry? Nobody could accuse you of being stupid," he said with the slight smile that only comes with victory. If he knew the rage of his guest, this lunch would not have been as cordial as it was.

*   *   *   *

The light tap on the door startled Bobbi as she moved to her side window to see Ellias Manuel standing at her door. Marko had been gone less than a week and here he was. Ellias was not wasting any time.

"Ellias.... What a surprise," Bobbi said, opening the door.

"I was in the city and I just had to pay a visit. Is it alright?"

"What do you think? Come on in," she said obviously pleased.

His red Jaguar convertible was pulled into her side drive. Ellias could have and probably did have the most desirable women in Columbia. It was flattering that he came to see her.

"Would you care for a drink?" she asked.

"Yes.... Do you have rum?"

She smiled as she got up to get it.

"On the rocks, please," he said.

"So what brings you to town?" she asked. Her hemline was well up her thigh.

"Business.... So much of my business is in Bogota. I may be seeing a lot of you," he said with his dignified smile.

"I hope so. I love company, especially from handsome, wealthy men."

"I'll be in town for several days. I hope we can have dinner a time or two," Ellias said.

"Sounds good," Bobbi said. She was getting a bad case of cabin fever.

"How about this evening?" he asked. "I need to go to an appointment in a few minutes. I could come by about seven? I know of a good place downtown, very good food, excellent atmosphere, and fine entertainment.... What do you say?"

"I'll be ready," she said with a smile. They exchanged a few more pleasantries and Ellias left with a quick peck on her cheek.

*   *   *   *

Jake stared across at the cold gray water of the Atlantic Ocean as he sat on the rail chair at the Third Avenue Pier. It was a warm December day in Myrtle Beach. Temperatures were expected to get into the high sixties. The long pier had five anglers at the moment, no tourists. Jake had been out a couple of hours and he had not seen anyone catch a fish. Joe Lane stood next to him staring across the water.

"How's Jane doing?" Jake asked Joe. Jane was Joe's wife of many years. She had battled breast cancer and with the aid of surgery had seemed to be getting through it.

"She's fine. Doc says they got it all. She'll have another checkup next month. Things are looking up."

"Good."

"So... are you coming?" Joe asked.

"What are you talking about?"

"Next Saturday, dumb ass. You remember... for dinner? Do you have any brain cells left?"

"You're talking in two weeks, right, the Saturday before Christmas?"

"You can actually count to two. I'm impressed," Joe said with a smirk.

"I think we can make it. I'll have to check with Sally. I'll let you know."

"By all means, wimp. Check with Sally."

"She thanks you."

"I'll bet she does. By the way, I wouldn't bring Sally if I were you."

Jake looked at Joe and wondered what was coming next, a wisecrack no doubt.

"The girl wants me, Jake. I can see it in her eyes. I don't know how much longer I can hold her off." Joe had a way of spewing out garbage that no thinking person could possibly believe and at the same time he said it like he totally believed it.

"I've noticed that," Jake said, playing along. "Do you have a spare room? Maybe she can just move in. I'm sure Jane would understand."

"Jane is used to women throwing themselves at me. The poor girl has had a hard life."

He finally said something that Jake could believe, the hard life part that is.

A sudden monstrous pull on Joe's line flipped his pole up into the air. The grip end of the rod seemed to be suspended in space right in front of Joe's bugged-out eyes. He gasped and then made a desperate grab for the base of the pole. He managed to get two knuckles around the butt of the rod as he desperately fought for control. His hold was precarious as it started to slip away. "Son of a bitch!" he yelled as he swatted at the fading pole with his free hand.

His grab for the pole was too little and too late as he watched his two hundred dollar rig sink into the cold Atlantic waters.

Jake looked at him with his mouth open not knowing what to say.... For the life of him he couldn't get the smile off his face. Finally he said, "Damn, you almost had him."

Joe looked at Jake like Jake was the neighbor's cat that had just landed on the Christmas ham. "Son of a bitch," Joe growled so loud that it caused two women who had just ventured onto the pier to abruptly turn around and hurry off. "Shut your damn mouth.... Don't talk to me, asshole," he spat in his wild-man, wide-eyed, rage as he pointed his battered, crooked, dirty, finger at Jake.

Joe promptly grabbed his remaining stuff and stomped off the pier, muttering, and cursing and slamming everything in his path, including the small folding chair that the portly, Melinda Jones was resting her ample rear-end on. Pulling herself off of the deck, she pitched a mullet carcass, striking old Joe, square in the ass. She kept starring, and he kept walking.... Thank God!

Jake, hoping the monster would return, hung around till dark without getting a bite.

*   *   *   *

Ellias Manuel picked Bobbi up at 7:05 P.M. It was a beautiful summer evening in Bogota. Bobbi wore a short blue skirt and white blouse. It was a good match for Ellias' red Jag convertible. He pulled to a stop in front of the Hombre Club. Once inside they were escorted to a quiet corner booth. They finished their meal just as the band began to play.

Ellias was the consummate Latin ladies man. A wealthy refined, gentleman, who was both passionate and exciting. Every woman in the club cast admiring glances his way while every man admired his date. The band played on with a strong Latin beat and the dance floor was filling up.

Ellias drank rum on the rocks and Bobbi enjoyed several potent frozen daiquiris and was feeling a little tipsy. She loved his company. Like Marko, he made her feel very desirable.

"You are the most alluring woman in here tonight," he said. The place had over a hundred women present so it was quite a complement.

"And you are a silver-tongue devil," she said. "Beautiful women are your specialty."

"I am no stranger to women this is true... but you are a special prize. Marko is a lucky man."

She blushed and continued to sip her drink. A young man came up and asked her to dance. She looked at Ellias and he waved her onto the floor. After a couple of dances, she joined Ellias again at his table.

"You're a good dancer," he said.

"Tall slim women are supposed to know how to dance," Bobbi said.

"I suspect you're good at a lot of things," he said with a smile. She waved her finger at him in a "naughty boy" manner.

They drank and danced the night away. He dropped her off at her place shortly before midnight. He did not ask if he could come in. She might have taken him up on it.

* * * *

Larry Holder stared out his back door. He set the beer down that had grown warm in his hand. He had to slow down on the drinking. His life had consisted of a drunken or grass induced stupor for a long time. Before Bobbi left, he smoked grass every day. Since she left he replaced the weed with the bottle.

He wondered if he would ever see Bobbi again. A part of him hoped not. He spent hours remembering how things used to be when things were better. The painful near past was strangely less clear. "Photographs show the laughs recorded in between the bad times, happy sailors dancing on a sinking ship," the words of a John Prine tune go. The human psyche has that ability, to forget the painful or at least not dwell on it and remember the good.

He'd entertained the idea of killing Marko, but what would that really accomplish? Rather than killing him, Larry had another plan, a plan that could mean his own death. He was considering going through with the blackmail scam. The account was set up in Costa Rica. Why not use it? Bobbi was no longer in the picture but so what? She had apparently long forgotten about the whole thing. For all Larry knew, Marko was taking care of her somehow.

What did he say? Larry thought. *'She pursued me,'* that's what the *asshole said*, he remembered. The thought of her going after him ate at his insides. The original plan was to get the access codes to the computer files at the Barn. There was more than enough information in those files to send Marko, Mona, Harone, and the Mob from Baltimore up the river for a long time.

Bobbi screwed up that plan in more ways than one. Plan B needed to be put into affect. The codes would have helped but they were not crucial. What did Larry need the codes for? The information he already had would be enough to squeeze them. He was in it from the beginning. Either Marko would meet his demand or he would go to the authorities.

The payoff would have to be quick. The Marianno Family would be called in immediately from Baltimore. It would not be wise to give them enough time to establish their network. They had a way of resolving problems in a hurry and he didn't want to be the cause of their happiness. As bad as things were, and they were bad, he was not ready to die, at least not yet. He would hit fast and hard and get lost. He needed to play it cool until he struck.

He should have been a little more cordial to Marko than he was during their luncheon meeting. He just couldn't bring himself to do it. It was hard to be nice to someone who was banging his wife. Be that as it may, he had to do better from here on out. He would make his move sometime after the first of the year. Until then he would be Mr. Nice Guy.

Larry went to the refrigerator and looked at the contents: a half a case of beer, a bottle of catsup, a stick of butter that had been there who knew how long, and a half a jar of dill pickles. "This won't do. It's time for this boy to get his act together," he muttered to himself. If he was going to be dodging Marko and the Mob, he would have to be at his best.

He took the beer to the sink and dumped it all down the drain. Dumping the beer hurt but it didn't hurt as much as flushing his bag of grass down the commode. That really did hurt. "Damn it!" he said as he headed out the door for a walk. "I got to get out of here," he said to himself.

For the first time in many years, certainly in his adult life, he was actually trying to take control of his life. He went to see Sam and Marie Conner. He needed to be with friends tonight. *Maybe Ted will come too,* he thought.

*   *   *   *

"You're very sexy for a man your age," a busty widow named Martha said to Jake as they were dancing at the Saturday dance class. Sally was dancing with a robust man on the other side of the room.

"Thank you. I try to stay in shape," Jake said to the less-than-attractive woman who obviously was available anywhere, anytime. Feeling obligated to return the complement, he said, "You're quite appealing yourself."

With that little bit of encouragement the massive redhead thrust her hips into Jake so hard he thought he was going through the plate glass window. "I got to have you, baby," she said hotly to him. "I want to take you places you've never been before," she said.

Where's that... the zoo? Jake thought. He didn't have the guts to say it; this woman looked mean. "My girl's right over there," he finally told her as if she cared.

"She ain't got enough meat on her bones to satisfy you. You ain't had a woman until you've had a big woman," Martha said. She was an authority on the subject.

Jake was surprised she was not disrobing right on the dance floor. She was uglier than sin but it was flattering that she was so hot for him. He did all right with women but it had been a while since he had affected a woman like this. In fact this was the first time!

Mercifully the dance ended and he found Sally at his side. "This is quite a guy you got here," Martha said, discreetly patting Jake's behind. "Yes, sir, quite the dancer," she said licking her ample lips.

"I told you that you would love learning to dance, darling," Sally said with her perky smile. She had been a cheerleader forty some years before and she still had that contagious exuberance for life. Standing next to Martha she looked like a damn movie star.

Jake took Sally by the arm and said to Martha, "Thanks for the dance. I'll see you next week." Martha stared at him with wide-open eyes and a big hungry smile on her face as Jake raced to the door with Sally.

"Are there any sailors in town?" Jake asked Sally as they got into her car.

"I don't know. Why do you ask?"

"Never mind," he said looking in his rear view mirror at the fading dance school.

CHAPTER 12

THE SATURDAY NIGHT CHRISTMAS PARTY at the Hanslow Plantation was going as expected. Mona was dressed to kill and Marko was making crude remarks to half the women present.

The gathering included: all the employees at Droughbrigh Country Club, several business associates, numerous dancers masquerading as upstanding young businesswomen, four or five outright call girls, and Monty Purcer. Not counting the Grounds Barn crew there were thirty-nine people at the party.

Sam and Marie Conner arrived early. Sam was in a tux and Marie wore a beautiful black evening gown that Marko and several of his cohorts couldn't keep their eyes off of. Ted Miller looked quite dapper in a sports coat and black turtleneck. His girl friend of several weeks, Nancy Tuttle, wore a smart gray suit. Ted was a happy boy. Larry Holder was alone and wore a tux.

Salloa had his usual bright blue robe with a big white star on the back. Most people thought he had been brought in to be the comic relief for the evening. He felt like it.

Gina Lacky was the best-looking woman in attendance. She wore a short baby doll maid outfit and spent the night telling drunk men "no" as they waved one-hundred dollar bills in her face and tried to pinch her amazing posterior.

The resident juvenile delinquent, Billy Pasko, had britches on that seemed to be buckled about half way down his thigh. He also sported a ring on the tip of his tongue. Mom and Dad were proud.

Herndon Jones and his lovely wife, Stella, were two of the most dignified and gracious people in attendance.

"I can see why you don't wear that thing to play golf in," Ginger said. She was the stunning forty-year-old grill cook at Droughbrigh who had a figure that didn't know what quit meant. She liked to wear clothes to show it off. Her tight, knee-length red dress was doing just that this evening.

Jake's cover didn't seem to be working with Ginger. "Yes. It would be a bit restricting," he said. "Have you been at Droughbrigh long?"

"Five years," she said. "Before that I was a dancer in town. I've known Marko a long time. He gave me a job out there. I like it. I was getting a little too old to dance. It's hard to compete with the young girls."

"I would imagine that you could still hold your own," Salloa said.

"I don't know about that... time marches on."

"Quite a spread here," Salloa said, hoping to keep the conversation alive.

"Yes it is," she no sooner said when a local attorney came and took her by the arm and escorted her to a corner love seat.

Oh well, Jake thought, *justice prevails.*

Across the room Larry chatted with Mona as Marko joined in.

"Larry... I hope you're enjoying the evening," Marko said. "I know it's hard under the circumstances."

"Yes sir. I'm doing all right. Each day gets a little easier. I appreciate your concern," Larry said. He had determined to be nice to Marko - the calm before the storm so to speak. Marko was pleased. He nodded in appreciation and moved on. Larry chatted another moment with the lovely Mona and went his way.

"You want a drink?" Gina Lacky said, offering Jake the last daiquiri on a once full tray.

"Twist my arm," Salloa said, picking up the last glass.

"I'd like to belt a few of these bastards," Gina said. "They talk to me like I'm part of the entertainment. Hopefully Marko's got a stripper getting ready to jump out of a cake or something. I'm tired of these assholes groping me. They need a diversion."

"Tell me about it. The women treat me the same way."

Gina smiled. "I just want to be treated as if I'm a person and not as a piece of meat.... They could learn a few things from you."

"My thoughts about you are not always honorable... I'll have to admit," Jake confided.

"I forgive you," she said as she grabbed Jake's drink and took a healthy swig before handing it back. "If the cops came in here they wouldn't know who to arrest first."

"Did the Paskos invite a few criminals?"

"Where you been, man? I'm not sure what this crowd is up to but I can assure you it's no good."

She might be right for all Jake knew. He really hadn't given it any thought. He didn't care where the money came from as long as he got paid. He assumed that the golf club was doing well. It was always busy when he was there. Here he was, the so-called "private eye," and the maid was more perceptive than he was.

She took another drink from Jake's glass. "You won't see this crowd at the Chamber of Commerce meeting.... See that couple over there?" she said pointing to a distinguished-looking couple standing near the door.

"I see them," Jake said.

"Mafia.... I'd bet your life on it."

"My life...? You are a brazen hussy."

"Ain't I though?"

"Mafia?" Jake said, shaking his head. "I think you're getting just a little paranoid."

"And I think you need to wake up," Gina said, taking one last drink before heading for the kitchen.

Mafia, Jake thought shaking his head and smiling. Suddenly a stunning blond in her early fifties grabbed Jake's elbow and looked at him with a knowing smile.

"I just love a spiritual man," she said with a sultry voice. "Mona is so lucky to have you." The girl just dripped with seduction and money, a combination that Jake was a long-time sucker for.

"Yes, my dear. The spiritual is the true reality," Salloa said. He was getting good at this.

"Isn't it though?" she said, drawing even closer to Jake. "Mona told me your name is Salloa.... I love that name."

"Thank you, and your name is?"

"You can call me Fanny."

Jake choked just a little bit when she said that.

"Is there any way you could work me into your schedule for a private counseling session?" she asked.

If I'm still breathing I'll be there, Jake thought. "I'm sure I can. What's a good time for you?"

"Monday morning about ten. Will that be alright for you?" she said.

Needless to say Jake said that it would be fine. He didn't even have to check his schedule. He got her pertinent information before she moved on.

By this time Ted Miller was standing next to Salloa. Curiosity got the best of him and he asked, "What the hell are you supposed to be?"

"I'm Mrs. Pasko's spiritual advisor... Salloa is the name, and yours is?" Jake asked, extending his hand to Ted.

"Ted Miller, I work at the Club. I'm in maintenance." Ted shook his drink and asked, "So what exactly does a spiritual advisor do, walk around and read the Bible to Mona? God knows she needs it."

"The Bible's a fine book. It's just one of many books I use.... And no, I don't just walk around and read passages. I try to capture the essence of the moment and pass that knowledge on to my clients," Salloa said.

"And you get paid for that... amazing," Ted Miller said.

"Ted... you better introduce me," Marie Conner said as she walked up. Marie was being her usual bubbly and good-looking self.

"Marie, this is Salloa... Mona's spiritual advisor," Ted winked.

"Oh, neat," she said. "How did you get into that kind of work?"

"The gods spoke to me, my dear. That is all I can say. It just happened."

Sam Conner stuck his nose into the conversation. "Are you associated with the Marat Hola group?" he asked. "I used to live next to a group of them in Virginia Beach. I liked having them around. They wore robes like yours."

"They're fine people," Jake said. "My beliefs are my own. I have obtained enlightenment from many different sources."

"No one could accuse you of being close-minded," Sam said with a smile.

That's for sure. Salloa talked several more minutes to the Grounds Crew and moved on into the night.

*   *   *   *

The Christmas holidays came and went. Jake was given a couple of weeks off from his private eye duties, Marko made a meager attempt at being a family man, Mona went on enjoying her massages from Monty, and the Grounds Crew kept on doing their thing.

In Columbia, Bobbi Thimpkin, formerly Bobbi Holder, was enjoying her new life. Marko called once a week and they planned their upcoming meeting in February. Bobbi was seeing Ellias Manuel every week and he usually spent the night. She rightly guessed that Marko wasn't saving himself for their next meeting.

Larry got through the holidays escaping with most of his sanity. He had managed to stay off the bottle, and except for New Year's Eve, he hadn't smoked any weed. He had things to plan and needed to keep a clear head.

One thing he needed to do was come up with a new identity. A friend in Wilmington knew someone who knew someone who might be able to help him out. He made a day trip to the port city and came back with a complete set of papers identifying him as Jerry Uller. The little exchange cost him thirty-five hundred dollars. It was part of the price of doing business. Most likely he wouldn't be able to claim it on his taxes.

The bank account in San Jose could be accessed by card so the name he went by was inconsequential from a money standpoint. He called Manuel Dalca at the Domingo Bank just to be sure there wouldn't be a problem. There was not. Evidently changing one's name was a common occurrence at Costa Rican banks. A person could have a thousand names. They didn't care. The name or names the account was opened in was the key. Dalca did ask about Bobbi. Larry told him she was fine.

The first Saturday in January would be the first of the large shipments coming into the Barn. Larry's plan was to partake in the first load on Saturday and the first exchange on Tuesday. On Wednesday, his day off, he would leave town and send Marko the blackmail note to his mailbox at the Dortshire Townhouse. Larry would lay low out of town somewhere until the money had been deposited in the offshore account. In the meantime he would be a model citizen.

*   *   *   *

The Porter Transport truck backed into the Grounds Barn. Ted Miller waved John Browner back as the large panel struck came to a stop.

"Where's Bobbi?" Browner asked, obviously missing her tight jeans and long legs.

"She went bye-bye," Sam Conner said as he signed the paperwork that Browner handed him. "Any problems at your end?"

"Not a drop. PT is a well-oiled machine," Browner said.

"Piece of cake," Sam said walking away.

"What do you mean she went 'bye-bye'?" Browner asked. Sam kept walking.

"Gimme a kiss, baby," John Browner said to Marie just loud enough for her to hear.

"Kiss this," she said, pointing to her butt.

The unloading went well. They were able to move the doubled amount of grass easily into position behind the computerized door. The truck pulled out at its usual time. There were smiles all around at the Barn table.

*   *   *   *

"Unbelievable," Marko's brother Harone said. "We should easily clear a million a month. That should keep us both in wine and women."

"Only the best, my brother, only the best," Marko said. "No problem then with La Capa?"

"No problem," Harone said. "The boys are pros. The best I've ever seen."

"Have you spoken to Theo?" Harone asked.

"Not yet. I was going to wait until the pickup Tuesday." It was always a little unsettling to talk to Theo Marianno. Their relationship had been a good one but, after all, he was a Mafia boss. Killing was as normal to Theo as fertilizing a fairway was to Marko. To Marianno it was just part of doing business, as Marko was acutely aware.

"He should be pleased," Harone said. "It could not have been smoother. Let me know what he says."

"I'll let you know."

"How's your work crew managing? They've had a hell of a few months.... What about Bobbi's husband, Larry, wasn't it?"

"He's doing surprisingly well. I have to commend him. He's being closely watched. So far so good."

"That seems rather odd," Harone mused.

"They have had problems for years. It may be a relief for him, too. I know it was for her."

"When will you see her again?"

"February. I'm planning a trip to Bogota. I miss her. She's so hot. I've not had a woman like her."

"You're a lucky man, Marko. Does Mona know anything about her?"

"Not a thing. She just thinks I'm doing my usual whoring."

"I need to get your play book. You have a good thing going."

"You do well yourself. I've seen your women."

They both laughed and chatted a few more minutes before hanging up.

CHAPTER 13

THE LETTER WAS SIMPLY ADDRESSED:

Marko Pasko
48 Ave North Unit 16
Myrtle Beach, SC

It read:

The party is coming to an end. I have played your game long enough. I'm no longer in the area. I want ten million dollars deposited to international account number: 400123-204B-002. I want it deposited no later than 11:00 A.M. Eastern Time, January tenth. If the money is not in the account on or before that time, the Myrtle Beach Police Department, and the Federal Task Force on Drugs will be paying you and the little woman a visit. If I get any indication that you are coming after me, I will blow the whistle and you will be going to prison. If you think I'm bluffing, try me.

It's one thing to trap us in your damn mess at the Country Club, but it's quite another to drive my wife away. Let's just say that this is my way of getting even.

Incidentally, the whistle will be blown on Malpass Trucking as well. They need to keep things cool. I'm sure you'll keep them informed... Theo... isn't it? You might want to touch bases with Harone.

Bobbi has nothing to do with this. I wish she did but she doesn't. So wherever the hell she is, leave her alone!

Have a nice life, Marko - give my regards to Mona,

Larry Holder

*   *   *   *

The first Thursday evening in January, Jake was in position at Marko's Dortshire townhouse with camera in hand. He recorded Marko arriving with a busty blond dancer barely out of high school. She helped herself to a drink and was unbuttoning Marko's shirt as he thumbed through his mail. The personal letter got his attention.

"Damn it, that bastard!" he screamed as he pushed the girl aside causing her to fall.

"What the hell's your problem?" she yelled.

"Shut your damn mouth," he said as he sat down and read the letter again. "That bastard is going to die!"

The girl stared at him with wide-open eyes. "Maybe I'd better go," she said, grabbing her purse.

"Yeah, maybe you better just get your little-ass out of here," he said. The girl picked up her purse and jacket and hurried out the door. Jake was surprised to see her leave so soon.

Marko dialed Harone's number. He answered on the third ring.

"We got trouble," he said as he read the letter to his brother.

"Find the bastard and kill him," Harone said. "Where could he be?"

"He sure as hell ain't hanging around waiting for a bullet, I can assure you of that," Marko said.

"Have you called Theo?" Harone asked.

"Not yet," Marko replied.

"You have to call him. He's got to know about this."

Marko had to agree with that.

"Where are you now?" Harone asked.

"I'm at the townhouse. I had a girl over. She just left."

"I'm driving up," Harone said. "When I get there we'll call Theo. I'm walking out the door now."

Marko poured himself a straight shot of whiskey and sat down in his recliner. He needed to think.

*   *   *   *

Larry Holder paid cash for a room at Holden Beach. It was thirty miles or so up the coast into North Carolina. It was a quiet place consisting of weathered beach homes owned by wealthy and not-so-wealthy East Coast residents. Many of the dwellings were for rent. This time of year most of them were vacant.

A Wilmington realtor turned him on to the Holden Beach area. He told the manager his name was Hank James. He would stay until the money was deposited - less than two weeks. There was no need to use his new documented name, Jerry Uller, for this temporary stop.

He had cash on hand to last a few weeks. If Marko didn't come forth with the money, he would blow the whistle and go about his life as the poor Jerry Uller. He couldn't see that happening. Larry figured he was either going to end up dead or rich. He preferred rich.

He shaved off his beard and cut his hair before going to a local barber for the final touches. It had been twenty years since he had been clean-shaven with short hair. Even his friends at the Grounds Barn would have to take a second look if they saw him on the street.

Nothing to do now but bide his time.

*   *   *   *

Jake filmed Harone's arrival at nine-thirty Thursday evening. Marko was tanked by the time his brother arrived.

"Well?" Harone questioned as he walked into unit sixteen.

"Well, what?" Marko said, returning to his chair.

"Any more news?" Harone asked.

"I gave you the damn news. He's got us by the balls. That's the news, end of story."

"No idea where he's at?"

"He didn't leave a forwarding address.... Can you imagine that?" Marko said, rubbing his throbbing head. "I called the assholes he works with, nothing. He didn't show up for work today. That's all they know," he said, spilling the drink that was in his hand all over his pants.

Harone walked to the bar and poured himself a tall glass of whiskey. "Make the call," he said as he took a seat across from him.

Marko drew a deep breath and dialed the number.

"Ophelia," he said, "this is Marko. Is Theo there? I need to speak with him." A moment later Theo Marianno came to the phone. Perspiration was pouring down Marko's forehead.

"What is it?" Theo said.

"One of my people has turned on us.... Larry Holder, he works at the Barn. He's blackmailing us."

"What the hell are you talking about?"

"I'm talking about blackmail, Theo. He says he wants ten million deposited in an international account by the tenth or he's going to the cops."

There was silence on the other end. Few people had ever dared to doublecross a Marianno and none had lived to revel in it. "I'm coming in tonight.... Remee will drive me."

"But..." Marko started to say as Theo hung up.

"He's coming in tonight. We need to go home.... I haven't told Mona yet.... She just might be a little pissed."

"Not the best day of your life," Harone added.

They gathered their jackets and drove to the plantation.

Jake noticed the somber expressions on the men's faces as they left. He packed up his camera and went home.

* * * *

Harone and a drunk Marko stumbled into the living room at the Hanslow Plantation where they found Mona reading a Spillane paperback.

"Harone," she said, half-greeting and half-questioning. "What happened to you?" she said looking at Marko.

"Not a good night," he said, slumping into an easy chair.

"What's going on?" she asked, looking from one to the other.

"We got a problem," Harone said. He looked at Marko and they both waited for him to speak.

Marko was almost too drunk to speak. It was very poor timing for a drunken stupor. He had to get his wits about himself. He gathered himself and began to speak. "We've been doublecrossed."

When he didn't say anything else, Mona asked, "By whom, damn it?"

"Larry Holder," he said flipping, his hand in the air. "Larry Holder."

"Larry Holder?" Mona questioned.

"One and the same," Marko said. "He wants ten million dollars deposited in an offshore account by the tenth." He looked at her with a drunken grin.

"What...? Are you kidding me? He's always been a great employee. We've never had any trouble out of him," she said, walking around the room. "This doesn't make sense.... Is there trouble between him and Bobbi?"

Harone looked at Marko, who was staring at the floor. Marko didn't say anything.

She stood above him and demanded, "What's going on? What's going on with Bobbi?"

He didn't say anything and continued to look at the floor.

She got down into his face. "What's going on? Speak to me damn it.... Are you screwing her?"

He didn't say anything and continued to look at the floor.

His non-answer was the only answer she needed. In a flash she slapped his red face with a nearby serving tray, tumbling Marko's drunken body onto the living room rug. She leaped on top of him, pounding her fists into his nose and eyes as he struggled to pry her away.

Harone jumped into the middle of the fray and placed his chest between the two lovebirds.... He took the worst of the beating. After several minutes of struggling, the three of them laid on the floor, winded, disgusted, and bleeding.

"You asshole," she finally managed to say. "Why didn't you stick to your damn whores?"

"Good damn question," he stated, staring at the ceiling fan through blood shot eyes. The fight had been beaten out of him.

The three of them lay panting on the floor. They felt like they had spent five minutes in a blender and had just been dumped on the carpet.

"Where is he now?" Mona said after getting her wind back.

"We don't know," Harone said.

"Where's the bitch?" Mona said, rising and looking down at Marko's fixed glassy gaze.

He braced himself for another onslaught and said as calmly as he could, "Columbia."

She screamed a primal scream and wrapped her hands tightly around his neck. He grabbed a handful of her hair in each hand and tried to separate it from her head.

Harone, still winded from the last assault, let them fight. He had put up with their shenanigans for too many years. He was too old for this crap.

After several minutes of cursing, rolling, pulling, and slapping, they both gave up. Mona looked at him with murderous eyes and said, "Why don't you just go down and live with the bitch? It would suit me just fine. I ain't gonna be lonely." They all knew that was true.

"Will you two assholes shut up...? I'm trying to sleep," the resident juvenile delinquent said, suddenly appearing in their midst.

"You little shit," Marko growled as he groped to his feet and lunged for Billy. Marko tripped over a coffee table and slammed his nose into the lush carpet causing a flowing stream of blood as Billy made his escape.

"Oh, piss," Mona said as she threw Marko the box of tissues that was on the table.

"We're going to have to call Theo," Mona said. "He is going to be furious." She walked to the window and stared into the night. "I don't know what he's going to do."

"He'll be here in a couple of hours," Marko said, sitting in a chair and wiping the sweat and blood from his head. He was drenched with perspiration.

"Great...that's just great, and I haven't even baked a damn cake," she said as she sat beside Marko, holding her head in her hands. The three sad figures sat in silence and waited.

CHAPTER 14

SHORTLY PAST THREE IN THE MORNING, Remee and Theo Marianno pulled around the circle to the front door of the Hanslow Plantation. Mona met them at the door.

"Theo... Remee," she said, opening the door. They tipped their hats and walked in.

Theo nodded at Harone and went straight to Marko, who was standing to meet them.

"What's going on?" Theo Marianno asked him as he threw his hat onto a chair.

Marko looked terrible, his eyes were swollen, claw marks where on his face, and he reeked with foul odor. "The bastard stiffed us," he said.

"He stiffed you," Theo said with an odd smile on his face. "I take it that you have no idea where he is?"

"None," Mona said. "His coworkers don't know anything. Do you need anything to drink, coffee?"

Remee nodded as Mona left the room.

"How did this happen?" Theo asked Marko.

"He wanted out," Marko said. "His terms were ten million."

Theo laughed while looking at the others. "Pretty lousy terms, I would say. He's a dead man.... What kind of terms are those?"

Theo set his coffee cup down and looked hard at Marko. "Shit like this just doesn't happen out of the blue.... I'm going to ask you again. How did this happen?"

Marko swallowed hard as perspiration poured from his forehead. "His wife recently left him.... He thought I had something to do with it," he said, haltingly. "He's pissed."

"Why does he think that?" Marianno asked, with his muscle Remee standing right behind him.

"I had been seeing her for a few weeks," he said, in a barely audible tone.

Theo Marianno looked at him with a big toothy, sadistic grin. "She works for you. They both do, right?"

Marko Pasko nodded that was true.

Theo Marianno turned his shoulder toward Remee as if to say something. Instead he uncoiled a vicious slap across Marko's face. He followed it with a series of blows that backed him across the room and up against the wall.... Marko knew better than to retaliate. His face was stinging, swollen, and bleeding. The old man stepped aside and Remee stepped in landing two quick punches, the first to his face and the second to his stomach. The assault left him unconscious on the floor and drooling blood. Mona gasped and kneeled beside him. Harone turned away and vomited on the coffee table.

*　　*　　*　　*

Salloa tapped on the front door and waited.

"Hey," Gina said in a subdued manner as she led him in. The girl liked Jake – not surprising, considering the wackos who called Hanslow home.

"And how's my girl this morning?" Salloa asked.

"You don't want to know," she said, as they breezed toward the back veranda. "A couple of heavies showed up last night," she said in a hushed tone. "They beat the shit out of Marko. I don't know who these people are, but Mona and Marko are scared to death."

Jake couldn't believe what he was hearing. "You're kidding. So there is just two of them?"

"Yeah, an older guy and a young thug. I think they're Mafia."

"What would the Mafia have to do with the Paskos?"

She shrugged her shoulders and said, "I don't know. They're up to their butt holes in something. That's for sure. They're all huddled back in the office. They have been there for two hours." She fiddled with a window blind for a moment deep in thought. "Marko looks terrible," she said in not much more than a whisper and with fright in her eyes. "They really beat him.... They beat the hell out of him and he's back there kissing up right now. You figure it.... They ain't the boy scouts. That's for damn sure."

Something heavy duty was going on. Gina had said something about her suspicions at the Christmas party. Jake had not given it much thought. It looked like she was on to something. Dirty money was probably involved. Just why and how much was the question.

The shuffling of feet and voices were heard as the group walked through the house and came upon Gina and Salloa. She was right; Marko looked terrible and Mona was as white as a sheet. The old man was five feet eight inches and stocky. He was accompanied by a young man in his late twenties, six two and muscular. They did not look festive.

Obviously embarrassed by Jake's presence, Mona said, "Oh...I forgot, Salloa, my spiritual advisor, comes on Fridays."

"Get him out of here," the old man said.

She quickly took Jake by the arm and walked him to his car. Looking over her shoulder she said, "Don't come out here for a few days. I'll call you and let you know when it is all right. As you can see we have some company." She started to walk away.

"I can see that," Jake said. "Is everything ok? I mean, is there anything I can do?" He didn't mention how bad Marko looked, but it was obvious in his voice that he was concerned.

"No thanks.... Everything is fine," she said, while wrenching her hands and looking back at Jake. "Marko fell last night. He had a little too much to drink. He does that sometimes."

"Did you want me to continue to stake out the townhouse?"

"Yes, do that. I will call you when it is safe... I mean, when it's good to come back here. I'll be in touch," she said, as she turned to walk back into the house.

"Ok," Jake replied. "I'll talk to you soon." She didn't hear Jake's last sentence. She was already in the house.

He started up his old truck and drove away. Something strange was going on here and he was going to find out what it was.

*   *   *   *

Gina prepared lunch for the Paskos and their agitated guests. After dinner, the group retreated back to the office.

"Call her now," Theo said.

Marko dialed Bobbi's number as Mona gave him a cold stare.

It was 10:00 A.M. Bogota time as Bobbi picked up her phone. "Hello," she said.

"Bobbi... it's Marko," he said, cupping the receiver.

She could tell by his voice that something was wrong. "What's up?"

He was sure that she knew nothing about what Larry had done, but he had to ask. "Larry has screwed us.... He's

145

demanding ten million by the tenth. Do you have any idea where he might be?"

The air went from her lungs. *Oh my God! He did it even without the computer codes,* she thought. She composed herself and said, "I have no idea, Marko.... I can't believe he would do something like that." That was certainly the truth in her mind, at least not without her help.

Marianno motioned for Marko to press the speakerphone button.

"He has taken off and we don't know where. I thought maybe you would have some idea," Marko said.

"Not really. He's got relatives in Ohio.... He would not put them in danger by going there," she said as an afterthought. "He hasn't been in touch with his Navy friends since we've been married.... I don't have a clue. I guess he's holed up somewhere."

"And you have no idea where?"

"None."

"He said he wanted the money put in an international account. We think it's a Costa Rican account. Do you know anything about that?"

Terror came upon her. She felt the walls closing in around her. If the bank talks in San Jose she would be dead. Dalca promised the account would remain confidential. Anyway she cut it her life was taking a dramatic change for the worse. She regrouped and managed, "Costa Rican account? I have no idea."

There was an eerie silence on the other end. Marko had to be figuring *"How could he have an account that obviously had to be opened in Costa Rica without her knowing about it?"*

They will certainly check the airline record of their trip to the Bahamas, she thought. The noose was tightening around her neck.

"We're in a bind here. We have to find him," Marko said. Killing him would be the only remedy when they found him. Marko knew it and so did Bobbi.

"Where are you?" Bobbi asked.

"I'm home."

"Are you alone?" she asked.

"Mona is here, along with Theo Marianno and his driver. We're all very concerned."

"I guess everybody's listening?"

His silence answered her question.

She was very aware who Theo Marianno was. It would be one thing trying to slip away from Marko, quite another to elude the Mafia.

"I wish I could be of help, Marko. Is there anything I can do?"

Marko looked at Marianno with a "what should I tell her?" look.

"Tell her to come home, now," Marianno said in no uncertain terms.

"She ain't staying here," Mona said sharply as she turned and walked out of the room.

"You need to come home now," Marko said to Bobbi. "Call the airport and get the first flight out."

"Marko, I just don't know if I can pick up just like that and leave. I love it here," she said, desperately trying to buy some time.

"It will be temporary, Bobbi. I need you here now. You must understand. Call the airport. We'll be expecting your call," he said.

"Ok... I'll call now."

"Good. Let me know your flight information. We'll be here waiting." He replaced the receiver and shrugged his shoulders. "She's gonna call now." No one really believed it.

*   *   *   *

Bobbi set the phone down on the receiver. Her breath was quick and her mouth dry. She grabbed her purse and sat at the kitchen table frantically looking through her purse. She found the card that would access the account at the Domingo Bank. She stared through the window toward the serene Fucha River and contemplated her next move. She took deep breaths trying to remain calm. She had to think clearly.

Flying to Myrtle Beach was not a good option. The thought of a hopping-mad Marko with his Mafia sidekicks meeting her at the airport was not an appealing one. She could only bluff them so long.... Staying in Columbia was not an option. Ellias Manuel had too many contacts in Columbia. She could never stay hidden here.

She could catch a flight to San Jose and meet with Manuel Dalca. He could hide her and also insure her that her identity on the account would remain confidential. She decided against that option. Most likely Mafia goons were already there or at least on their way. Dalca said it would remain confidential. She had no choice now but to trust him. She would call him soon. The money should be deposited in three days.

A part of her wanted to get up with Larry. Her heart went out to him. She doubted if he wanted to see her. Her gut feeling was that he was somewhere in the vicinity of Myrtle Beach. He might even still be in town. He was just that brash.

She made up her mind that she would find her way back to the Myrtle Beach area and try to find him. She would not take a chance with a plane. Traveling by plane, she could be easily traced.

She would try to sail by ship out of Barranquilla. She could arrange passage with cash in the port city. Life and death could be bought with money from the streets of Columbia and especially in Barranquilla. Certainly she could arrange passage on a ship. Hopefully she could gain passage to somewhere on the Gulf Coast of the U.S. She had to be cautious. Ellias Manuel would be involved very soon in her search.

She packed her suitcase and called one of the numerous private taxi services in Bogota and contracted the driver for a one-way ride to Barranquilla. She was gone within the hour.

CHAPTER 15

THEO MARIANNO ORDERED thirty-five mob underlings to the beach area with orders to look for Larry Holder. They combed the Carolina beaches from Wilmington to Hilton Head and a hundred miles inland looking for any clue to his whereabouts. Their orders were to kill on sight, no questions asked. Despite the manpower, it was like looking for a needle in a haystack.

Marianno had made it clear to Marko and Mona that the bulk of the money would come from their means, whatever it took. It could mean mortgaging their home and the Droughbrigh Country Club. He didn't much care. The parties involved would much prefer a dead Larry Holder. With Holder dead, the account could be frozen, giving the Marianno lawyers time to figure out how to get the money back.

By late Friday afternoon, after extensive monitoring of the airports, it was apparent that Bobbi was not coming in. Calls to her Bogota dwelling went unanswered. Marianno placed the call to Columbia.

"Hello," a sleepy voice said on the other end.

"Ellias... is this Ellias Manuel?" Theo asked.

Ellias shook the cobwebs from his head and eased out of bed, being careful not to wake the woman sleeping beside him.

"Yes, this is he.... And to whom am I speaking?"

"Theo Marianno from Baltimore."

"Marianno... is there a problem?"

Theo went on to explain the blackmail dilemma and Bobbi's failure to fly to the states. She was apparently on the run.

"We need her apprehended and delivered to us," Theo said. "We don't want her harmed. We know that she has not flown out of Colombia, at least not using the two names that we know of. Could she have flown out another way, maybe using a different name?"

Ellias knew that in Columbia everything was negotiable. An airline ticket for someone as alluring as Bobbi could certainly be arranged. Whether she realized that much was another question.

"I've got my sources. I'll do some checking," he said.

"Could she drive out or sail out?" Theo Marianno asked.

"Driving would be difficult. Going by ship would be more likely. I will check my contacts in Barranquilla."

"Time is of the essence," Theo said.

"I understand. If she is still in Columbia, we will find her. I can assure you of that."

The phone conversation ended and Ellias slipped back into bed. Tomorrow he would find the pretty Ms. Bobbi. He felt certain that she was still in Columbia.

*   *   *   *

Larry Holder enjoyed a coffee and Danish as he scanned the morning paper from the patio at his well-kept rented dwelling. It was a warm sunny January day reaching into the mid-fifties. The few tourists present this time of year were thoroughly enjoying this unusually pleasant weather and the low off-season rates that went with it.

Typical of small coastal towns, Holden Beach had very few motels. Most rentals were like the unit that Larry was in - a personal dwelling that could be divided into two to four rental units or as one large house for an extended family. Larry was holed up in a duplex with the other half not rented.

He settled in with food enough to last him the next few days, long enough for the money to be deposited and a few days to spare. Larry figured the Marianno family had thugs scouring the area. The quaint Holden Beach community would not be an exception. He was right.

The black sedan eased slowly down the ocean drive, stopping at every possible contact point. The beach only had a few stores and two open real estate offices. They said they were looking for their cousin who was staying somewhere in the area. Larry had contracted for his unit three weeks before from a realtor in Wilmington thirty-five miles away. That fact plus his changed physical appearance would for the time being serve him well. The sedan came and went in the quiet beach town. Larry knew nothing about it.

The past six weeks had been the worst stretch of his life. He spent too much time wondering about her. What was she doing? Who was she with...? That was the one that really hurt. Was she still seeing Marko? He had no way of knowing. He would get his revenge. Marko would pay. Blackmail was less risky than murder, and the reward so much sweeter. Besides, Larry was not the murdering type.

He knew from the beginning the danger he was in. He was under no illusion about that. The reality of the danger involved was setting in. He could deal with the danger he was in, that was his own doing. The danger his actions had put Bobbi in was another matter. As bad as the events of the past weeks had hurt, he did not want her harmed.

The account the money was to be deposited in could certainly put her life in jeopardy. It was supposed to be secure, but how secure was it? Could the bank be bought or intimidated into releasing information? If they divulge the holders of the account, Bobbi's life would be in grave danger.

"Why didn't I think of that?" he asked himself as he stared across the Atlantic. "I should have known better than that." If she knew by now what he had done, which she probably did, she would be terrified and on the run. He hoped that she did know, otherwise she would certainly be apprehended by Marianno's thugs.

Tears came to Larry's eyes. He was afraid for himself and for Bobbi. For the first time since he was a child, he bowed his head and asked God for help. He wept like a baby for two hours. Somehow on that sunny January morning with the Atlantic breeze blowing in his face, Larry Holder became a new man.

*   *   *   *

"Mr. Dalca?" asked a tall lean businessman in a tailored pin-stripped suit accompanied by a large burly thug in a worn brown suit.

Manuel Dalca looked up from his desk where he had been going through a mass of paperwork before his next appointment. "Yes," he responded, eyeing his two intimidating guests.

The Marianno family attorney, George Mason, handed Manuel his business card and proceeded. "My clients, a Mr. Theo Marianno and Mr. Marko Pasko, have instructed me to inquire about an account in your bank."

"Those names are not familiar. Are you sure they have accounts at Domingo Bank?"

"It's not their account, but rather the account of a close associate."

"Their associate should be the one checking on the account," Mr. Dalca responded. His suspicions were starting to be aroused. He had seen this game played before.

"We see a problem with the account. There may be funds involved with the account that could prove grievous to my clients."

"I'm sure you are aware, Mr. Mason, that we pride ourselves in our confidentiality when it comes to our customer's account. When an account is opened here it remains a private matter. We have the full backing of our national authorities when it comes to these things. To operate otherwise would be detrimental to our international interests."

"My clients, Mr. Dalca, are not individuals who... how should I say... are not overly concerned with the law. They are concerned with protecting their interests." He reached into his shirt pocket and handed the account number to Manuel Dalca. "I would appreciate it if you could pull up this account for us."

Manuel took the piece of paper and looked at the two men. "I can pull up the account, of course, but I will pull it up for my own information and not yours."

"Please," George Mason said in a way that expressed "that would be good and do it right now."

Mr. Dalca excused himself and stepped to a monitor in the lobby. "Larry and Bobbi Holder, Myrtle Beach, South Carolina." He scratched his chin and remembered the young couple. He smiled when he recalled Bobbi's long legs and jacked-up skirt. "Maybe some future negotiations will be in store with her," he mused to himself. He tucked the information into his pocket and went back into his office.

"It is a valid account number. It will remain confidential. You must understand," Manuel said.

Attorney Mason leaned across the desk with his thug hovering over his shoulder and said, "A large deposit will be made to the account on the tenth. Once the deposit is made, my clients insist that the account remain frozen."

Dalca looked at the two men and leaned back in his chair fiddling with his pen. "I take it your clients are the ones making the deposit?"

"Correct."

"If they are all that concerned, than why make the deposit?"

"That's my clients' business. The money must not be withdrawn from the account."

Mr. Dalca rose from his desk and looked at the two men. "The integrity of this bank is my business.... Gentlemen, I am a busy man with an appointment waiting. I have expressed to you our banking policies. If you do not want the money withdrawn, then I would suggest that you don't deposit it. Please..." he said, pointing them to the door.

George Mason rose and looked coldly at Dalca. "If the money is withdrawn from this account, my clients will hold you personally responsible. Unlike the good people of Costa Rica, they are not nice."

The two visitors left the office and Manuel stared at the door behind them. He had been in this position before. It was not one he enjoyed but it came with the territory. He was paid a hefty salary for his position at Domingo Bank for exactly the situation he was faced with now. Being an international banker brought many friends and many enemies. He had no choice but to maintain the integrity of the Holders' account.

When things get tight, the clients always call. Sometimes, it was to his advantage to portray that he could keep their account secure only with his own heroic efforts. It was especially helpful when dealing with attractive women. The truth was that if he succumbed to outside pressure and compromised the name of the Costa Rican banking community his own people would kill him. His clients didn't need to know that. He expected to hear from the Holders soon, hopefully Bobbi.

*　*　*　*

"This better be good. You interrupted my beauty sleep," Rudy Rogers said to Jake, as he sipped coffee and devoured a biscuit at the Beach Deli.

"I obviously woke you up way too soon," Jake observed.

"You could use a few more winks yourself," Rudy said. "What's this about? I'm a busy man. I've got crosswords to do."

"Strange things are developing with my job at the Plantation."

"Don't tell me... they've found out that Salloa is a fraud?"

"A few of them might be on to that. That's not the deal though. How much Mob activity goes on around here?"

"Mob as in street punks, or mob as in Mafia?"

"Mafia."

"You think the Paskos are involved with the Mafia?"

"I don't know.... So, there is some Mafia activity around here?"

"I'm retired from the Myrtle Beach Police Department. Remember, Jake? Contrary to what you think, officers of the law have to use their head for more than a hat rack. With all the sex business down here, don't you think that just maybe the Mafia might be involved?"

"Sex business?" Jake asked.

"Yeah, sex.... You remember sex, something men and women do?"

Jill Arthur strode by them with a coffeepot. Both of their sets of eyes were glued on her lovely sway as she headed down the counter.

"It's all coming back to me," Jake said.

"Nothing like a visual," Rudy agreed. "Why do you think they are involved with the Mob?"

"A couple of strange house guests at the Hanslow place for one thing - an old guy and a young thug. It looks like the young guy beat the hell out of Marko. Not only that, the old guy seems to be running the show. I mean he is telling the Paskos what to do in their own house."

"Maybe they're disagreeable relatives?"

"I don't think so. Gina Lacky, the foxy maid I was telling you about, she's been telling me for months that they're tied in with the Mafia."

"Gina, the maid?" Rudy asked.

"One in the same. The lovely Gina Lacky, total knockout."

Rudy stirred his coffee and looked up at Jake. "Tell you what, old pal, I think you better stick to doing your Swami routine instead of trying to bring down the East Coast crime syndicate."

"I just love older men," Jill said in a pouting manner standing in front of their table and holding a coffeepot.

Jake looked at her, then looked at Rudy, and then looked back to her. "What you trying to do, give me a heart attack?"

"Of course not, I love you guys," she said, bending over their table and refilling their coffee while showing just a little bit of cleavage. She twisted a way with a wink and a smile.

"Where the hell was she thirty years ago, Jake?"

"Kindergarten.... So you think I should forget about the Paskos and the Mafia?"

"That's right, forget it. If they are involved, you don't want to know it. Sometimes being dumb and happy is the best way to go."

"Coming from you that means a lot," Jake said.

They finished their meal and sipped their latest refill. "The people live like kings, Rudy. Have you ever seen the Hanslow Plantation?"

"I've driven by, but I haven't paid much attention."

"Take a look sometime. You won't believe that spread. I know owning a golf course pays well, but that place is a little much. Another thing, these people aren't exactly what I would call workaholics. The party is what they're interested in. I know that's the deal with Marko, and I think Mona is playing the same game. If they don't give a damn about running the golf course, where is all that money coming from?"

"Look Jake, I don't know what you want me to do? I can't go to the vice squad because they've got money and somebody beat the old man up. I've got to have something a little more substantial than that. If they are involved, you better be damn careful, that's for sure. If they get wind that you are suspicious, they'll kill you. They don't play."

"I'm not stupid. I just want to keep my eyes open. That's all," Jake said. "The only thing I can figure is that something must be going on at the golf course. There're no red flags at the house that I've seen. I don't know about Droughbrigh. Maybe we can nose around out there."

"We?"

"Yeah, you know, when we're out there playing. We can keep our eyes open. Hell, we spend half our time in the woods looking for balls anyway.... You did say you wanted to work for me?"

"I don't remember that."

CHAPTER 16

BOBBI PEERED THROUGH HER WINDOW at the Bananka Hotel on the hot Colombian summer morning. The money was to be deposited into the bank in less than twenty hours. She checked the balance the night before. No new money had been added or withdrawn. If Larry could not be found, the Paskos would pay the money. She was confident of that. They had too much to lose. They would do what they had to do. They could kill Larry later, and probably her, too.

She examined the business card in her hand belonging to Manuel Dalca at the Domingo Bank. It would be mid-morning in San Jose. She made the call.

"Manuel Dalca," he said.

"Mr. Dalca.... This is Bobbi Holder. My husband and I talked to you in October."

Manuel smiled as he leaned back in his chair, "Yes, my dear. I remember you well. How may I assist you? And please call me Manuel."

She mustered up her nerve and went on, "I'm in a jam. Our account will have a large amount deposited tomorrow, and the depositors are not happy about it. I'm sure they are trying to track me down right now. They may approach you and try to get information about the holder of the account. I'm holed up in a hotel now. I'm frightened and don't know what to do."

"I'm glad you called, my dear. I'm sure I can help. There has been inquiries concerning your account. I had a couple of visitors yesterday in fact."

Bobbi held her breath as Manuel Dalca went on.

"They wanted me to reveal the names on the account and to freeze it once the deposit was made. They went so far as to threaten me. They were quite intimidating."

"What did you tell them?"

"I told them that we must maintain the integrity of our accounts."

"Were they satisfied?"

"Those types are never satisfied," Manuel said. "You can be sure of that." He leaned back in his chair. "These cases put me in very awkward situations. You do understand. I am taking a great risk for you."

"I realize that," she said.

"Special compensation might be in order.... Do you know what I'm saying?"

She knew exactly what he was saying. He wanted sex. "I believe I do," she said.

"You understand that it is something that only you can do for me?"

"Yes."

"Where are you now?"

"I'm at a hotel in Barranquilla, Columbia. I've got to get out of Columbia."

"Who's after you there?"

"Every cowboy in Columbia, that's who. I'm afraid to leave the room.... Have you ever heard of Ellias Manuel?"

"Does not ring a bell."

"He's a business associate with the people who are upset about the account. He is also the top police officer in Columbia. I know him well, usually under much more favorable circumstances. He has contacts everywhere."

"Can you change your appearance?"

"Not hardly. Long-legged U.S. girls have a way of sticking out around here. It's not a hard place to get a date."

"Let me think about this," he said, rubbing his chin. Is there a number I can reach you at?"

"Call the Barranga Hotel at LM5-445-7890. Ask for room 606."

"Sit tight. I will call you this time tomorrow. Don't leave your room and don't worry about the money."

Putting down the phone, Dalca smiled as he contemplated the near future.

* * * *

"How much will be left?" Mona asked.

"A million and a half. The asshole is taking ninety percent of our investment money," Marko said, sipping a shot of whiskey. "The bastard won't live to enjoy it if it's the last thing I do."

"You can't keep your damn pants on and we're losing everything we've got," she said, giving a look of disgust.

"Like you're little Ms. Goody Damn Two Shoes."

"Have I cost us ten million, Marko?"

"Why don't we both just shut the hell up?" he said. "It's done, damn it. I can't change it now." Unfortunately they both knew he was right about that.

"I guess they've already moved the money," Mona said, looking at her watch.

"Should already be done.... He's moving an extra million just to cover capital gains." Marko rubbed his head. "We're getting robbed and I got to pay taxes on it.... I can't believe this shit."

"At least we got the extra dope money coming in. We should be able to make it back in a year or so," she said.

"Let's hope so," he muttered half to himself.

*   *   *   *

Stella Lane was working alone in her Wilmington real estate firm when the large sedan pulled up outside. She heard the door slam and looked up to see two imposing figures walking through her door.

"May I help you?" she asked.

"Have you seen this guy?" the roughest looking one asked as he slid a picture of Larry Holder across her desk.

She recognized the picture to be the young man to whom she had rented a Holden Beach property to a week before. The recognition on her face did not escape the notice of the two men.

"Seen him before I take it?" the burly intruder asked.

"If I did I wouldn't tell you," she managed enough courage to say as she handed the picture back.

The thug jerked the phone lines out of the wall. "You're going to need to learn to cooperate," he said.

"What...What the... What are you doing?" she said indignantly.

The big guy sat on the desk, crowding her to the point that she was forced to scoot back in her chair. "I'm going to ask you just one more time.... Where's he at?"

She was on the verge of fainting and past the point of thinking straight.

"Look, lady, we don't want to have to hurt you. But if you don't come clean about this clown's whereabouts, we won't have a choice.... Where is he?"

She trembled as she fumbled through her filing cabinet looking for the folder in question. "He's at Holden Beach," she said in a barely audible fashion. "662-B, Ocean Drive."

The big ugly goon smiled a toothy grin and said, "Now that wasn't so bad was it?" His accomplice took a roll of duct tape and began wrapping the tape around her feet. "Don't fight it, sweetie.... He gets real nervous."

She sat perfectly still as he went about his work wrapping her feet, hands, and finally her shoulders to the straight-back chair she was sitting in. He secured the leg of the chair to the leg of the heavy desk. A bandana was tied around her head to keep her from shouting for help. With a wave, they were out the door and on their way for the thirty-five-minute drive to Holden Beach.

Pure luck caused Larry to notice the long black sedan easing down Ocean Drive and gliding to a stop in front of his unit. He had just walked by the front window on the way to the kitchen. A quick glance of its two menacing occupants and his throat went dry. He eased out the back door and quickly navigated the back steps. He maneuvered his way to the rear of the adjacent house to the north.

Moments later the intruders had circled 662-b. One was knocking on the front door while the other stood under the deck directly below the back door. They had their guns drawn. Amazingly, they hadn't seen him leave.

Larry carefully sneaked his way down the beach past three more houses. He watched as the large man standing at the front kicked the door in and went inside. Larry saw his chance and crossed the street heading away from the water. He went over two streets to a parallel street that ran along the waterway and toward the bridge that led out of the beach area. The bridge was five miles away.

Just ahead he spotted the "Mom and Pop" convenient store with a payphone outside. He called a Wilmington cab company for a pickup at the store. He stepped inside and ordered a hot dog and a drink from the pretty young girl who was alone in the store. Larry took a seat on one of the two counter stools and waited for the cab, constantly watching the front of the store. The quiet beach was practically void of commercial establishments. If his pursuers happened to notice this little store, they would certainly stop.

The girl was attractive and in her mid-twenties. She wore a UNC Wilmington sweatshirt. Working a crossword, she occasionally cast a wondering eye at Larry as he ate and stared out the window.

"Refill?" she asked when he finished his fountain drink.

"No thanks," he said.

"I take it you're expecting someone?"

"Yeah... I called a cab."

She went back to her crossword and looked up. "Are you on the run? You seem kind of nervous."

"No, I'm fi-..." he started to say when the black sedan pulled up. "Shit!" he exclaimed. "Where can I hide?"

"Back here!" she exclaimed. "Behind the counter."

He ducked behind the counter and hid directly below her and under the counter. Her thigh was leaning against his shoulder.

"Has anyone come by here, a tall lanky white guy?" the beefy man asked in a stern manner.

"Haven't seen anyone.... It's been really slow."

"We need to look around," one of them said as he came around the back of the store.

She turned around and leaned up against the counter with her hands folded. She was doing her best to shield Larry from his view.

"I told you there wasn't anybody here.... It's been slow as hell."

They continued to look around. The man directly across from her handed the girl a card. "If you see anybody that fits his description, call me. It'll be worth something to you," he said.

"No problem," she said as he walked back around to the front of the store.

Both men stood at the counter, looked around, and shrugged before exiting out the door and speeding off.

"There they go," she said as Larry slowly raised up from behind the counter.

"Thanks," he said. "You saved my life."

"They look serious. Why are they looking for you?"

"You're better off not knowing."

She gently put her finger on his chest and said, "I get off in an hour. I got an apartment in Wilmington. You will be safe there for a few days."

It was an offer he could not refuse.

*　　*　　*　　*

"Hello," Bobbi hesitantly said from her hotel room in Barranquilla. It had to be Manuel Dalca. He was the only one who knew where she was.

"Bobbi...? Manuel here. I have made some contacts and have arranged for you to leave Columbia."

She sat up in bed and listened carefully.

"A friend who owes me a favor often sails to Rio with a stopover in Barranquilla. He has room on his vessel for you. He routinely ports in Barranquilla, so there will be no red flags, a totally routine trip.

"He tells me the best time to board will be late at night. He suggested three in the morning. Girls come and go at that time of night in the dock area. They will assume you are a call girl. You'll have to dress the part. Will that be a problem?"

"I can handle it," she said.

"Good.... A cab will come by and pick you up at exactly 2:50 A.M. Walk directly out of the hotel. The cab will be waiting for you. Carry very little luggage, in fact, put everything you need in your purse. Call girls don't usually carry a suitcase. You can shop in Rio."

"Ok."

"Another thing, the money is in the account. It was deposited within the hour. Ten million to be exact. Don't touch it now. We will access it when you get to Rio. I will be there a day after you arrive. I'll be on Latino flight number 754. It arrives at noon, 12:10."

"I'll be there.... Who owns the boat?" Bobbi asked.

"His name is Oscar. The boat is called 'Pot of Gold.' We'll tell the cab driver where it's located. He will assume that you are a prostitute going on a call."

"When will I get to Rio?"

"Four days... you will leave in the morning about nine. The ship is small. The crew will consist of Oscar and eight or nine mates. It might be a good time to catch up on some sun bathing. You might want to pickup a bathing suit if you don't have one."

"I have one."

"Good. Just lay low today. Don't leave the room unless you have to. From what I've gathered, Mr. Manuel has many eyes in Barrangquilla. You must be careful. Do you have any questions?"

"No.... I'll be ready for the cab in the morning."

"Good.... I'll see you in Rio in a few days. As you can imagine, I am very much looking forward to it. Until then, be careful."

"I will," she said. "And thanks."

"You can thank me in Rio, my dear.... Goodbye," he said, hanging up.

She put down the receiver and stared across the room as the summer breeze gently blew the curtain across her open window. The sounds of traffic moving and street vendors drifted her way as she contemplated the adventure ahead. "Rio de Janeiro," she said to herself. "Wow!"

CHAPTER 17

WHEN HER QUITTING TIME APPROACHED, Larry went to the girl's car, laid down in the back seat, and waited. The girl's name was Elaine Coy. Ten minutes later he heard a car pull up. Someone got out of the car and went into the store. Two or three minutes later, Elaine got into her car and cast a smile back at Larry hunkered down in the rear seat.

"Those guys scared the hell out of you. That's for sure," she said, starting up the small foreign car and speeding off.

"Are you married?" she asked.

He didn't answer right away and finally said, "I guess I am." He said it in such a way as to convey it was questionable at best.

"Life's a bitch," she said half to herself. Ten minutes later she pulled to the curb and stopped in front of a small beach house. "I got to pick up Daisy," she said.

"Daisy?" Larry questioned.

"My baby," she said.

"Oh," Larry said, shaking his head.

Three minutes later Elaine got back in the front seat. Daisy immediately peered over the back seat looking at him with the wonder that only a child can have. She was a beautiful girl of about three with pretty blond curls and big blue eyes. She could not take her eyes off Larry. "Hi, Hanks," she finally said in a dainty voice. He had told Elaine that his name was Hank James. The less she knew about him, the better it would be for her.

"Hi," Hank said. "Did you have fun today?" he asked.

"Yeah. I made cookies today. Mommy says you can have one after dinner. We have to eat our dinner first," she said with a nod and a sparkle. Larry could see Elaine's smile in the rear view mirror. She was one proud momma. Ten minutes later they pulled into her apartment complex.

"It might be a good idea if you sit up," Elaine said as they were pulling in to her apartment parking lot. "We don't need you looking too guilty, now do we?"

"Good idea," Larry thought.

She parked directly in front of her apartment and they walked straight in. "Set your bag over there," she said, pointing next to the couch. "Make yourself at home. I hope you like hamburgers," she said, looking over her shoulder.

Elaine moved off into the kitchen. Daisy plopped down in front of Larry with her box of toys and began to drag them out.

There was something soothing about spending the evening with this young mother and child. He loved children but he had long since ruled out the possibility of being a parent. His sad psyche had discounted the simple pleasures of a real family or his own little girl.

Elaine put Daisy to bed shortly after nine and settled down on the couch and positioned herself toward Larry.

"Want a beer?" she asked.

"*What a question?*" he thought. It wasn't long ago that he couldn't face another day without beer or dope. He wasn't about to get back into that scene. "No thanks," he said.

She got herself one and joined him again on the couch. "So what are you going to do now?"

"I'll be going soon. I need to do a little banking in the morning. Is there an ATM anywhere close?"

"There's a bank right across the street. About fifty yards from where you're sitting."

"Excellent," he said.

They sat in silence for several minutes. She finally said, "You seem really scared. Those guys are dangerous aren't they?"

"Very."

"I guess you're not going to tell me why they're looking for you? You don't seem like the kind of guy who would be mixed up with guys like that."

"Things happen, Elaine. Sometimes you choose your path and there is no going back."

"I know all about that."

"How's that?" Larry asked.

"Daisy's dad was a one-night stand. I got pregnant. I thought about getting an abortion.... I can't believe I even considered it. She's the reason I can face every day. It's funny how things work out. I thought getting pregnant was the worst thing that could ever happen to me and it turned out to be the best."

Larry could relate to that.

"So where's your wife?" she asked.

"I don't know. She left a couple of months ago."

"I'm sorry," she said. "Another man?"

"Yeah.... Originally anyway. After that, I think she just liked being free.... We had a terrible marriage."

"You seem like you would be easy to get along with."

"I'm a different person now. I was drunk and high all the time. It was my own fault that she left. What can I say?"

"So you quit getting high after she left? Most people fall apart when something like that happens."

"Tell you the truth," Larry said, "I thought seriously about killing myself. If it wasn't for my friends, I wouldn't have made it."

"So you went cold turkey?"

"Yeah."

"I noticed the New Testament in your pocket. Are you a Christian?"

"I guess so.... It's the strangest thing. I cried out to God for help a couple of days ago. I don't know... I just feel like he heard me. I mean... I feel different. I've never been a religious person. There was a testament in the place where I was staying and the manager said I could have it. Two days ago I would have never believed it. I haven't cracked a Bible in my life."

"I grew up in a religious family," she said with a faraway look in her eyes. "They disowned me when I got pregnant.... My daddy called me a whore," she said, turning away, tears forming in her eyes. "I ain't got any use for what they called 'faith.'"

They sat there for several minutes with neither one saying anything.

"I'm making it on my own now...me and Daisy. She's all I need. Two more years of school and I should be able to get a good job. I'm really a pretty tough cookie," she said, perking up.

"What are you taking?"

"Nursing. I'm getting some help – student loans. They're pretty steep, but I'll cross that bridge when I get to it.... Like I said, I'm a tough cookie."

"I can see that," Larry said, full of admiration for this young fighter. "I don't know why people act the way they do, Elaine. Sometimes Mom and Dad can forget that they made mistakes along the way, too."

"No doubt," she said.

Larry continued, "Two days ago I had absolutely no concept of religion. It's all upside for me. I have no recollections of religion one way or the other. From my viewpoint it just seems good."

They sat in silence several more minutes.

"What do your parents think of Daisy now? They must be thrilled."

"They've never seen her."

"You're kidding?"

"No."

"They've never called?"

"They don't know where I am. The phone's unlisted."

"You need to talk to them. As hard as it is to do, you need to forgive them. God will give you the strength to do it. I really believe that."

"Don't talk to me about God, ok.... Could you forgive your wife?"

Larry hadn't thought about it. To his surprise, in his heart, in the core of who he was, he could forgive her. He understood at that moment that God had really changed his heart. "I can forgive her," he finally said in not much more than a whisper, more to his own amazement than to Elaine's.

"I'm happy for you, Hank, or whatever your name is," she said with a smile, "but I just can't do that... not now." She got up to head for the bedroom, "I guess this means you're going to sleep on the couch?"

"I better, Elaine. I can't get involved with you. I'm trouble."

"Well, you're sweet trouble," she said as she pecked him on the cheek and went to bed.

Larry went to sleep with thankfulness in his heart and a prayer for things to work out for Elaine and Daisy.

*   *   *   *

Mona called Jake the night before the deposit was to be made informing him that there would not be a need for him to come to the Hanslow Plantation any more. He would continue to film Marko at the townhouse and report to her once a week via telephone. His pay would be cut in half. It was still the easiest money he had ever made.

The new arrangement gave Jake time to do a little snooping around Droughbrigh Country Club. A round of golf scheduled for Monday with Rudy would afford them an opportunity to investigate. In the meantime, he would relax.

Being the first weekend in months that he had not worked, Sally and Jake celebrated by taking a trip to Blowing Rock, North Carolina. The January weather was unusually mild. That along with low off-season rates made for a pleasant weekend.

Jake didn't have to tell Sally that she was special to him. She felt the same way about him. He was content when he was with her, whether it was sitting in the hotel room reading, or snoozing on a comfortable bench while she hit the outlet shops. They treated each other with respect and gave each other the room they needed to be themselves.

Marriage at this point was too complicated for either of them or their grown children. For the time being they just treasured what they had. In their minds, they felt halfway married anyway.

*   *   *   *

Bobbi had no trouble finding an outfit that looked like she could be a prostitute. In fact, most of her wardrobe could fit that purpose. At ten till three in the morning she stuffed as much as she could into her large purse and headed for the front door. The cab was waiting.

"Pot of Gold," she said as the cabby waved an "I know" wave.

"Need a discount on the fare?" the driver said with a heavy Latin accent and an admiring glance.

"Not tonight," she said.

He said something not understandable and drove off. Two minutes down the road he threw his hands up as a red flashing light came into view. His muttering to himself had not stopped. He eased his cab to where the police had the road barricaded. An officer came to the driver and they talked hurriedly for several moments. He shined his flashlight back in Bobbi's eyes. The light then dropped for a few seconds on her legs. The conversation between the officer and the driver became quite animated. The driver stepped out of the cab, came around and opened the back door, and motioned for Bobbi to step out.

The officer turned her toward the car and frisked her. He ran his hands all over, and in some cases, under her clothes. The backup officer laughed at the scene before him.
Satisfied with his groping, he pushed her back into the cab. With reluctance the officer waved them on. The terrified and enraged Bobbi trembled under her cool exterior.

The cab pulled to a stop at the deserted dock area. The streets were empty with only an occasional drunken sailor staggering down the street. Girls of the night were on every other corner even at this late hour.

She could see the small boat not fifty yards away. She paid the driver and quickly walked to the "Pot of Gold." Approaching the boat she was met by a lanky, chain-smoking man of fifty whom she assumed to be Oscar, the captain of the boat.

"This way," he said, leading her aboard and into a small room that consisted of a small bed and a chair. "Stay inside until we set sail. We will leave about nine. I will let you know when it's safe." He nodded and left her alone.

At eight the next morning, she was awakened from a surprisingly sound sleep by the muffled sounds of voices and the low rumble of an old diesel engine. Several minutes later she felt a slight shift of the boat as she pulled away from her moorings.... Bobbi was on her way to Rio! Thirty minutes later, Oscar knocked on the cabin door and told her it was safe to come topside.

The spectacular morning view took her breath away. It was a beautiful summer day with a slight breeze and cloudless blue sky. Oscar met her at the top of the steps as she stepped into the light of day. The Columbia skyline was barely visible on the western horizon.

"Morning, Missy," Oscar said. "I hope you slept well?"

"Yes, thank you," she said. The boat looked larger when it was tied up. The vast sea reflected how small the boat was. It was seventy yards long and twenty-five yards wide. The ocean was rather calm. The rolling waves gently rocked the boat side to side. The crew was all topside to check out their new guest. They were not disappointed.

"You must be hungry.... What may we call you?"

"Bobbi," she said. "A little something on my stomach might be nice."

"I'll have something brought up. The view is much better up here. I'm afraid we don't have much of a breakfast selection."

"Whatever you have will be fine, Oscar," she said. He hurried off to bring her a piece of bread and several items of fruit along with strong Colombian coffee.

The next several hours were spent meeting the deck hands and listening to tall tales concerning their supposed exploits with women. They were hoping that Bobbi would be impressed - amused yes, impressed, no. The Costa Rican men she had met so far were on the passionate side and these men were no exception. She was glad her quarters had a door that locked. She would need it.

CHAPTER 18

LARRY SLEPT WELL on Elaine's living room couch. Daisy woke him up early by tickling his ear and running to hide. He pretended like he was a sleeping monster. Daisy loved it. Elaine fixed bacon, eggs, and English muffins. She and Daisy were out the door by ten. Elaine gave Hank a sweet kiss on the way out. *This is getting more complicated by the second,* Larry thought as he watched them drive off. She expected to be home by mid-afternoon. Meanwhile, he had things to do.

He pulled a ball cap low as he stepped out the door. Though he only vaguely resembled his former self, he couldn't be too careful. The most striking difference in his appearance was his short hair and no beard.

The sky was overcast and the morning air chilled as he walked around the corner toward the ATM machine located across the street. The money should have been placed in the account the day before. The Paskos would have no excuse for not having the money in the account by now. If it wasn't in the account, he would place the call.

Two little kids pulled at their mother's sweater as she completed a transaction at the machine when Larry walked up. He looked at his card and waited. He noticed that "Manuel Dalca" was listed as his bank representative. Dalca told them that the account could be accessed from any ATM worldwide. *Let's hope he's right,* Larry thought.

He punched in his access code and checked the account balance. "Hot damn dog," he said as he saw $10,000,000 U.S. come up. He tapped in a withdrawal and watched as the machine counted out $10,000. This happened to be the maximum amount that Dalca said the machine could handle on any given transaction.

Larry walked several blocks to a nearby strip mall and called a cab. "Take me to a bank," he said.

"Which one?" the driver asked.

"Just need an ATM machine, go," he said, pointing away from the bank he just left.

The driver took him to banker's row near the mall and not far from the college. Larry withdrew $10,000 each from three different banks. He paid the driver and walked down the street with forty thousand in his pocket. He called two more cabs and reversed his steps. He was happy to find that each of the banks allowed another $10,000 withdrawal. He arrived back at the apartment with a cool $120,000 in his pocket. Elaine and Daisy would be home in two hours. He would not be there.

He took out a pen and began to write:

Dear Elaine,

I had to leave. It is too dangerous for me to stay. I don't want to do anything that would put you and Daisy in danger. I wish things were different for me now. I think we could have had something special. As it is, that's impossible. You're a great girl and I know good things are in store for you.

Don't give up on God. People let us down sometimes but Jesus never will.

Look in your coffee decanter. You might like what you see.

Your friend, Hank

P.S. – call your mom and dad. Daisy needs to know them.

Larry stuffed $100,000 and a note into the decanter. He looked up and said, "I like the way you answer prayers." Larry smiled as he called a cab to meet him down the street.

*   *   *   *

Jake frowned as he looked at the sports pages in the Beach Deli.

"Indians lose again?" Jill asked with a pout.

He looked at her and said, "What do you think?"

"I think you better start rooting for another team."

"Come on now... they were pretty good for awhile."

"Every dog has its day," Jill said. "I haven't seen your girlfriend lately. She dump ya?"

"She knows better than that. Guys like me don't come along everyday."

"Thank God for small favors," she said.

"I'm glad you don't mean that," he said, looking back down at the paper. "Talk about a waste," he said, laying the paper down. "I've spent so much time looking at the sports page over the years. I could have been doing something productive like writing a book or something."

"Yeah, Jake, that's what you need to do, write a book. You got to put me in it though."

"You can count on that, darling."

"Rated 'G', too."

"If I must."

"I started to write a book one time."

"What was it about?"

Jill sighed, "It was about a young girl who married a prince and everything was wonderful." She smiled and added, "It was fiction."

"You still seeing that guy... Raymond, wasn't it?"

She shook her head and looked off toward the street. "He said he needed space.... First decent guy I've met in God knows when, and he says he needs some space."

"Your prince is out there somewhere, Jill."

"You keep thinking that, Jake," she said with a wink as she went about her work.

*　　*　　*　　*

Elaine walked into her apartment with Daisy in tow. "Hank?" she said. There was no answer. She was disappointed to notice that his duffel bag was gone. There was something about Hank, or whatever his name really was, that struck a chord with her. "Another one bites the dust," she said to herself. She felt like crying.

Walking into the bathroom she saw the note taped to the mirror. She read it and went to the kitchen and opened the coffee decanter.

"Oh, God!" she said as she counted out the money and collapsed onto the floor crying. A note with the money read, "The money is yours. Don't be afraid to use it. - Hank."

"What's wrong, Mommy?" Daisy asked, hugging her mother and looking into her tear-filled eyes.

"Nothing's wrong, honey. Everything is great!" she smiled through tears of joy.

"Is Hanks gone?" Daisy asked.

"He's gone, honey. He was a nice man, but he just had to go," she said as she hugged her little girl while they both sat on the kitchen floor.

*   *   *   *

"Hello?" Marko said from the plantation.

"The account's been accessed," Theo Marianno said from his office in suburban Baltimore. "The son-of-a-bitch didn't waste much time."

"How much has been taken?" Marko asked.

"The bastards in San Jose won't say. The only information they'll give us is the account is open and it's been accessed."

"Did you talk to Dalca?"

"No... he's not there today. For some reason the asshole needed to take a trip. He's booked a round trip ticket to Rio to return in four days."

"You think he's planning on meeting someone? Maybe Bobbi has made contact with him," Marko said, thinking out loud.

"That's what I'm thinking.... He could be leading us right to her. He's got a penchant for female customers. I've got two of my men in the air for Rio right now. They'll get there before he does."

"What are you going to do with him?"

"Kill him of course... after he leads us to the girl. We told him to freeze the account. He doesn't respect us."

"What about her?"

"What about her...? The bitch is going to talk one way or the other."

"What are you going to do with her?"

"If my men find her, I'm flying to Rio for the festivities. She won't see the morning sun. So much for your girlfriend," Theo said in a voice as cold as steel. He didn't need to say that he would have his fun before he had her killed.

"Keep in touch," Marko said as he put the receiver down. Theo had already hung up.

He looked at Mona and shook his head.

"They don't play do they?" she asked, already knowing the answer.

Lifting his eyebrows he said, "They don't play."

*   *   *   *

The weather was calm for her four-day journey to Rio. The crew had treated her well. She had been propositioned by every one them except Oscar. They were good boys - just hot-blooded.

The day before they arrived, Bobbi took advantage of the sun in her swimsuit much to the delight of the crew. Humored by their catcalls, she spent her time thinking about the drastic changes that had taken place in her life. She was now just a few months removed from her former life with Larry where she was stuck in a descending marriage and working at the Grounds Barn.

She wondered how her friends were doing, probably fine. They were stable people, unlike her and Larry. They had been through a hell of a year - the mess with them of course and the terrible events concerning Hannah and Mike. She didn't believe for a moment that it was a murder suicide.

Her thoughts always seemed to come back to Larry. She hoped he was doing well. Being high all the time would not work well for his trying to stay undetected. There was the possibility he had already been found. If that were the case, he would be dead by now. If he was still alive, he would have taken out some money. It was the same old story, follow the money. Dalca would have that information when they meet up in Rio.

Manuel Dalca... now that was another matter. She found him moderately appealing. She would do her best to cooperate on this Rio fling. A few days and it will be over with. She figured it was a regular game he played. He did get her out of Columbia. She did owe him that much. Without his help Ellias would have found her by now.

Ellias, she thought with a smile on her face. *Now there's a piece of work - the best looking man I've ever seen, let alone dated.* Her life had definitely become more interesting during the past few months. *I wonder what Ellias is doing now?* she thought as she closed her eyes and heard the whistling of one of the deck hands. She gave him the finger and pretended she was dozing.

* * * *

Ellias Manuel scratched his head. Every police precinct in Columbia was on alert to find Bobbi. She was nowhere to be found. All the airports in the country had been strictly monitored. The air system consisted of numerous small runways that routinely flew drugs out of the country. Without an inside drug connection there would not be a passage out. He was quite sure she hadn't left by air.

Finding a way out by ground transportation posed its own set of problems. Navigating the rough terrain and dealing with the local thugs made it next to impossible.

The best bet would be by boat. Hundreds of boats leave from the coastal and river areas in Columbia. The majority of craft were never inspected. Her good looks could easily persuade a captain to take her on a pleasure cruise.

Ellias Manuel shook his head and said to himself, "What a shame." The gorgeous young lady waiting in his convertible would have to ease the pain.

CHAPTER 19

DEBRA COY LOOKED at her husband Ray sitting across from her at the breakfast table. Ray was a good man. He was a faithful Lutheran and a devoted husband. Their daughter Elaine had been gone a little over four years. Her departure had taken its toll on both of them. It showed more on Ray. They rarely spoke of her.

"I couldn't sleep last night," Debra said, interrupting the silence.

Ray didn't have to ask why, he knew why. She was thinking about Elaine, Elaine and her baby.

"Will she ever come home?" she asked with moist eyes.

"I don't know," was all Ray could manage.

* * * *

Jake and Rudy teed off at 9:10 Monday morning. It was a cold morning with temperatures not expected to get above the low forties. Droughbrigh Country Club was nearly vacant.

Jake started with three straight pars. One more and he would tie his all-time best streak. A triple bogie on number four gave him a big dose of humble pie.

"What's that over there?" Rudy said, pointing toward the Grounds Barn in the distance.

"If you hadn't been running your mouth I wouldn't have three putted back there," Jake said still fuming over the last hole.

Rudy shook his head. He had heard Jake's crying routine a thousand times before. "Over there, wonder boy, what's that?" he said pointing again toward the Grounds Barn.

"It's a maintenance barn, dodo. What did you think it was?"

"How many maintenance barns does this place have? We just passed one back there. You remember... you just bounced your ball off the tractor sticking out the front door."

"Oh yeah.... Good work, homey," Jake said. "Let's go take a look."

They wandered over that way with club in hand like they were looking for their balls. The building was sixty yards off the fairway. Anyone who had been watching them play on a regular basis could certainly believe that their balls could have been hit that far off target.

Ted Miller saw them approach the barn. He kept a cautious eye on the comical pair as they snooped around in the brush near the barn. He confronted them when it seemed they were in no hurry to move on. He was especially concerned when he saw Jake tug on the side door. "May I be of assistance?" Ted offered with a glaring look.

"Can't seem to find my ball," Jake said with a dumb look on his face. It was his natural look. Jake vaguely remembered Ted from the Christmas party at the Hanslow Plantation. Fortunately, Ted did not seem to remember him. It must have been that blue robe.

"You think your ball went through the door?" Ted asked with a glance toward the door that Jake had just pulled.

Jake just threw his hands up and said, "Just clowning around. We can't play golf very well so we get our kicks by just doing whatever dumb thing comes next. We don't know what we are going to do from one moment to the next." The stupid look on Jake's face was his best defense.

Ted looked at the dynamic duo and figured they were just stupid enough to be telling the truth. Intelligence was not a requirement to play golf at Droughbrigh. "This isn't a playground, boys. This is a work area. The course is that way," he said, pointing toward the fifth fairway. "You see those white sticks over there?" They nodded that they did. "Out of bounds. If it's hit here...leave it.... Understand?"

"Yeah, I know," Jake said. "I hit my ball over here. I thought I could find it.... Is this a maintenance barn?"

Ted Miller looked at him real hard. "No.... This is a roller rink.... Of course it is. What did you think it was?"

"Yeah, it looked like one," Jake said. "So, there's this one and the other one off number four?"

"Yeah, so?" Ted said, getting a little annoyed.

Jake shrugged, "It just seemed a little odd. Most courses just have the one barn."

"So you decided to have a look around?" Ted went on trying to figure where these two clowns were coming from.

"Like I said it's no big deal. We're just out here goofing off."

"Well goof off somewhere else, boys. This area is off limits.... Bye," Ted said in a voice that conveyed an order as opposed to a suggestion.

"You bet... no problem," Rudy chirped in as he grabbed Jake by the collar and turned him toward the fairway. "Have a nice day," he said over his shoulder.

Ted looked at the two comical characters as they ambled off toward the short grass.

"He's hiding something," Jake said, looking at Rudy as he threw a ball down in a plush spot.

"He might be," Rudy agreed.

"There's something in that damn building that he doesn't want us to know about."

"Hit the ball, Einstein. He's still watching us."

Jake took a ferocious swing with his two-iron and knocked his ball eighty yards down the course and into the only bush in sight.

"Damn, you're good," Rudy smiled.

"Shut up," Jake said as they hopped on the cart and sped off. "I'm not counting that one."

"Idiots," Ted Miller said to himself as he went back to his work.

*   *   *   *

Larry worked his way from Wilmington to Charlotte during the course of the next two days. He traveled by bus from town to town. Once in the towns, he would call a cab and make his rounds to the banks. By the time he stopped in Raleigh, Burlington, Greensboro, High Point, Salisbury, and Charlotte, he had accumulated $550,000 - fifty-five stops at $10,000 each. Using his new name, Jerry Uller, he bought a one-way ticket for Quito, Ecuador.

He had never been there or known anyone who had. Years before he had seen a TV program describing the city. It was a city of one million situated on the equator and high in the Andes Mountains. Because of the altitude, the climate was very close to ideal year round. Twenty miles down the mountain from Quito was another story. There it was home to some of the harshest conditions on earth – hot as hell and a tropical jungle filled with cannibals, snakes, insects, and various other terrors.

"Bobbi would never consider Quito," Larry said to himself as he settled into his airport motel room for the ten-hour wait before his flight. His thoughts eventually turned from Bobbi to Elaine and Daisy. He smiled and went to sleep.

* * * *

The huge statue of Christ was just one of many awesome sights that painted the landscape as the Pot of Gold made its way into the port of Rio de Janeiro on a hot summer morning. The beach was lined with impressive skyscrapers that wove like a silver thread between the lush mountainous jungle and the aqua green South Atlantic.

Like many places, Rio was more beautiful from a distance. A close up view showed a city with massive crime, suffocating poverty, and overwhelming political, economic, and moral problems. It was a city perpetually caught in the fast lane. Bobbi stared at the sights before her and contemplated where this turn in the road would lead. Oscar came to her side and they leaned together over the rail of the vessel.

"It is beautiful," he said, looking straight ahead.

"Beautiful and frightening, too," Bobbi said, oddly feeling a cold chill cover her arms.

Oscar lit yet another cigarette and continued to look straight ahead. He had been to Rio many times. It was not a tourist city for him. The cargo would be unloaded during the next several hours. Tonight he would have dinner and a beer or two. Tomorrow the ship would take on a load of mahogany and return to San Jose. It was a familiar routine for the Pot of Gold.

"Where are you to meet him?" Oscar asked, knowing full well the price this trip would cost her.

"The airport.... His flight is due in tomorrow morning."

"Where are you staying?" Oscar asked out of curiosity. He had been a gentleman the whole trip and would continue to be.

"A hotel near the airport. When I get up with Manuel he'll take care of the arrangements."

Oscar continued to stare ahead. "That statue always grabs me when I see it, the statue of Christ. It reminds me of my failures but also it gives me hope. How does it affect you, my dear?"

Good question, she thought. She had been accused of a lot of things in her life, but being religious was not one of them. When she was a child, the church bus would come by and pick her up. That went on a year or two. It was more about her mother's sanity than it was for any sense of any pressing spiritual responsibility – a couple of hours of solitude. She didn't blame her mother for it. That was just the way it was.

"I don't think much about it one way or the other. It's pretty. I'm not very religious," she said just a little bit embarrassed.

He chuckled, "Everybody's religious, my dear. To not believe is a religious viewpoint." He pointed toward the approaching humanity. "There are ten million people in that great city, and every one of them has made something their god.... Do you believe that?"

She looked at him and smiled, "I never thought about it that way. But, yes, I guess you're right. I guess we all worship something, even if it's our own opinion."

"Not only pretty, but smart, too." He put his arm on her shoulder in a fatherly way as the ship eased into the Rio de Janeiro harbor.

The ship slipped past the famous beach areas of Copacabana and Ipanema. Eight cruise ships were tied up around the next corner. Two miles farther the commercial harbor came into view, no less impressive, but certainly not a resort location. The place reeked with a strong odor of dead fish and raw sewage. The yard was filled with workers, street children, vendors, whores, and drug addicts.

"Stick with me," Oscar told her as they stepped off the boat. "I'll take you to a cab."

They walked two hundred yards into the dockside market and a mass of humanity. A man leaning against a building chewing on a toothpick got Oscar's attention. He went to him and spoke briefly. A moment later the man went to the curb and opened the door on a beat-up compact car. He motioned for Bobbi to step in. Oscar explained to the driver where she was going and paid him the proper fare. He turned to face Bobbi, who was ready to step in.

"It's been my pleasure to have you with us these few days. You seem like a daughter to me," he said with complete sincerity.

Bobbi hugged him and said, "Thanks.... I'll always remember my days on the Pot of Gold.... I'll think of you when I see the statue."

"Don't think of me, my dear... think of Him," he said as he kissed her on the cheek. She stepped into the cab and was sped away.

* * * *

"He just got away!" Theo Marianno screamed into the phone in erupting rage. "Hell no! The son-of-a-bitch doesn't just walk away. He's probably still down there. Find his ass!" He slammed the phone down on the receiver from his Baltimore office and speed dialed Marko Pasko.

"Hello," Mona said.

"Let me talk to Marko," Theo said in his best gangster voice.

"Asshole," she muttered to herself, taking the portable phone to Marko in the other room. "It's your hero," she whispered, handing him the phone. "Theo," she whispered to his puzzled look.

"Hello," Marko said.

"You're a half million dollars down. He ain't wasting no time."

"Did you call the bank?"

"Just got off the phone not an hour ago...your money's dwindling fast," Theo said. "My boys had him outside of Wilmington, some hick place called Holden Beach. He must have seen them coming. The coffee in his cup was still hot for crying out loud."

"He must be still there," Marko said. "Are your boys still in the area?"

"They're still there. Who knows where that asshole is...? All I know is he's getting richer and you're getting poorer by the damn minute."

"What are they saying in San Jose about freezing the account?" Marko asked.

"They ain't talking. My boys will meet Dalca in Rio.... He's gonna find out that it's not wise to play games with Theo Marianno."

"Well, maybe we'll get lucky in Rio," Marko said.

"Let's hope so. He might be meeting her... your pretty Ms. Bobbi. It's payback time and he's there to collect. Dalca probably set up her escape."

"It's possible," Marko mused. "She's certainly desperate. Access to the money would be a must for her now.... So Mr. Dalca is a bit of a ladies man?"

"He thinks he is. My sources tell me it is not unusual for him to extract favors from desperate female bank clients. My guess is he's meeting up with her. If we can find her, we can use her for bait to find her husband."

"Do you think she's already in Rio?" Marko asked.

"She's somewhere. I'd say that's as good of a bet as any. We should have more information tomorrow. We'll catch the Holder bastard. When we do, I'll let you have the privilege of pulling the trigger.... I'll be in touch," Theo said hanging up.

Marko sat in his chair and withdrew a long breath. *What's next?* he thought.

CHAPTER 20

"TURN THE FLASHLIGHT ON," Jake said. "I can't see where I'm going."

"Have a little bit of damn fortitude. We can't turn the light on - we'll be spotted. Besides, there ain't no snakes in here. You're imagining things," Rudy Rogers said.

"Something crawled across my feet, damn it. If it wasn't a snake, what the hell was it?"

"Just shut up and keep moving," Rudy said. "We ain't gonna die in this swamp tonight."

Jake Brown and Rudy Rogers plodded their way through the thick marsh area that borders Droughbrigh Country Club just adjacent to the fifth fairway. It was 12:30 A.M. on a clear and cold January night. Jake had finally convinced Rudy that he should join him in his private eye shenanigans.

Risking possible arrest as Strand Private Eye's first employee was not overly thrilling to Rudy at the moment. Just six months removed from being one of Myrtle Beach's finest, now he was trespassing on private property and probably for no good reason.

The possibility that something was suspect in the maintenance building in question seemed slim. If it had anything to do with the Mafia, it would certainly be locked and might even be guarded by a non-cooperating Doberman. To top it off, Jake was floundering around in the brush and making enough noise to awaken half of North Myrtle. Rudy's guess was Jake was trying to scare the gators off. He was doing a great job.

Forty-five minutes of prodding and cursing found Jake and Rudy standing on the fifth fairway.

"We should have just walked through the gate," Jake said.

"Oh, yeah," Rudy said. "You'd be real popular in prison – too old for a date and too worthless to kill.... You have heard of motion detectors.... I can't believe that people actually pay you."

"Easy, cowboy.... You're working for me now."

"I guess I really have bottomed out," Rudy uttered as they eased the two hundred yards to their final destination.

Rudy did have the presence of mind to bring his contraband stun gun, compliments of a procurement officer buddy at the police department. The thought of dogs on guard made him more than a little nervous. He prayed to God that he wouldn't have to use it. Jake, walking immediately in front of him, did present a tempting practice opportunity. He rejected the impulse and kept on going.

The Grounds Barn was still and dark except for a single floodlight on in the front of the building. They rattled the brush and slapped a few trees to awaken the dogs. If they had to deal with dogs, it would be better if they had proximity to trees, especially trees with low hanging branches.... Apparently, there were no dogs.

They moved closer.... Jake was having a problem with gas, and it was getting on Rudy's last nerve since Jake was leading the way.

"Do you need to wipe?" an annoyed Rudy asked.

Jake turned his head around and said, "I'm nervous for crying out loud.... Give me a break."

"How about at least toning it down?"

"Whatever," Jake said.

They made their way through some brush and were standing next to the side door leading into the building. Rudy tried to turn the knob. It wouldn't budge. He could tell it was not dead bolted from the inside. He drummed the door with his fingers, still no sign of dogs. Rudy took a knife- like device from his pocket and began to work it ever so carefully in the keyhole.

"It's an impressive lock," he said. "It's not giving me much of a read."

"You think we can get in?" Jake asked.

"We can get in. It just might take a while," Rudy said as he continued to work the device in a workman like manner.

Jake was pleased with his new employee. He was more than a little curious about how his police training had taught Rudy the art of picking locks.

"Bingo," Rudy smiled, turning to Jake as the door swung open.

Rudy, not reveling in his victory, hurried in with Jake following. Beside the door was the box he was looking for. It was the alarm control center for the building. Rudy pressed the universal disarming sequence of 7756 into the keypad. He took a cable and shorted the detection lead to metal on the doorframe. The alarm disturbance light went out and they both breathed easier.

"Damn, that was close," Rudy said. "These things don't give you much time...no time for a screw up."

"Where did you learn to do that?" Jake asked.

"You don't want to know."

Probably not, Jake thought. They switched on the lights and looked around. The place was windowless and tight as a drum. For a working barn, it was surprisingly clean; no oil on the floor, no grass seed or fertilizer, and no lawn equipment. It was equipped with a couple of small tractors, a forklift, and a small wagon. A computer station sat prominently against one wall. A screensaver reading "Who's your daddy?" was running on the system.

Rudy tapped the computer keyboard. An "enter password" prompt came onto the screen. Rudy was not surprised.

"What seems odd about this place?" Jake asked from behind him.

"Other than the fact that it's cleaner than my living room, not much. It does seem odd.... Doesn't look like they're doing much work out of this place...weird," Rudy observed, turning away from the computer.

"That's what I was thinking," Jake said. "It could be a front for something... but a front for what? That's the million dollar question."

"Check that back wall out," Rudy said, pointing over Jake's shoulder.

Jake didn't get the connection, "How's that?" he asked.

"Everything else in here has something leaning against it, but not this one. Not only is there not anything against it, there's nothing on it... totally clean," he said, scratching his head.

Jake's curiosity was coming alive, "You think it's just a coincidence?"

Rudy raised his eyebrows as if to say, *"Who knows?"*

"Let's just say that it's not.... What purpose would it serve?" Jake asked. He felt the wall. It was solid and seemed permanent.

"There's something going on here," Rudy said. Starting at the front rollup door he paced off the steps to the back wall. It measured thirty-one steps. Out the side door he went with Jake on his heels. Starting from the front of the building he marched off forty steps to the back.

"There's nine yards of building behind that wall."

"Maybe there's a door in the back," Jake said. They circled the building. The only two doors were the rollup front door and the side door they entered by. They went back inside and walked to the wall.

Rudy looked at Jake and said, "It's a fake wall. There's a switch here somewhere or it's opened another way."

"What other way could there be?" Jake asked.

Rudy turned around and pointed toward the computer, "There, my boy... right there."

The computer, Jake thought, scratching his head. He just might have to give Rudy a raise... first thing next year.

They had been in the building almost two hours. They planned to try to gather more information from somewhere and come back later with a plan of attack. They turned out the light and reactivated the alarm. Jake pulled the door shut and it locked behind them. Their minds raced over the possibilities as they made their way back to the car.

*   *   *   *

Larry Holder arrived at Douglas International in Charlotte one hour before his flight. His business passport would allow him to stay in Ecuador twelve months at a time. He was nervous, though it seemed unnecessary; he had more I.D. on him than at any time in his life. Flight #4563 to Mexico City was on time. From Mexico City, after a one-hour layover, he would be on his way to Quito.

He boarded the plane and took a window seat. It was apparent that the plane would not be full.

His only luggage was in two carry-on bags. He would stay in the boarding area in Mexico City. He hoped his carry-on luggage would not be searched once he arrived in Quito. He hesitated in carrying so much money with him. If he was questioned, he had the necessary business material to back up his alibi about purchasing a golf course. In fact, he had an appointment set up. He planned to keep it.

Larry settled into his seat and began to read a section in John from his pocket New Testament. After a few minutes his mind drifted to thoughts of the recent events in his life. He thought about Elaine and Daisy, his friends at the Grounds Barn - most of all he thought about Bobbi. He couldn't blame her for leaving. He couldn't expect her to stay with a man who was drunk or stoned all the time.

What would she think of his new-found religion? In all the years of their marriage, he could not remember the subject of religion ever coming up.

He had forgiven her concerning Marko.... It was his bright idea.... She just took the ball and ran with it - the ball he handed her. She ran right out of his life. It was probably best for the both of them. He was going nowhere fast - she deserved better. He closed his eyes and slept.

The stopover in Mexico City was uneventful. Four hours later he was touching down on a runway that ran through the middle of Quito. He found himself on top of the world high in the Andes Mountains.

Quito was a dazzling, modern city resting on a mountain shelf, surrounded by some of the most rugged and beautiful terrain on earth. Snow- covered volcanoes punctuated the landscape. The cool weather and the rich black dirt on the mountaintop plateau made the city a haven that drew people from the surrounding area. The high altitude temperatures ran from forty to seventy-five year round compared with temperatures in the one hundreds in the tropical jungle just forty miles down the hill.

Larry walked through customs without being stopped. He hailed a yellow cab and was hustled off to the Holiday Hotel in downtown Quito. The streets were filled with smartly-dressed men and women. The women wore short tight skirts. *"Another disgusting destination!"* he thought. So long Larry Holder... hello Jerry Uller.

*   *   *   *

Bobbi's room had a magnificent view of the city. The ocean-side wall was solid glass from top to bottom. A view of adjacent high-rise hotels and the distant beach was afforded from her balcony. The tab per night was less than one hundred U.S. dollars.

She sipped her drink from her balcony this warm South American morning. She'd call a cab soon to take her to the airport to meet Manuel Dalca. Her early arrival gave her a chance to settle in. She loved her hotel accommodations.... She would not take her belongings with her. In her mind this had to be the best room in the city. Dalca would be so hot to trot, he wouldn't be picky. He would certainly want to keep her happy.

At 10:00 A.M. she stepped into a cab and directed it to Galeao Airport. She wanted to get there plenty early – she didn't need any surprises. She dressed conservatively in black slacks with a white blouse and sunglasses. She didn't want to draw attention to herself.

Arriving at the airport, she made her way through the huge concourse and found a seat in a lounge area facing the gate Manuel was to come through. The airport had more lounges than restaurants. The room where she waited had tinted glass that was impossible to see through. The morning crowd in the lounge was already half drunk. She ordered a daiquiri and waited.

Caution was a must in her mind. Dalca treated his dealings with the Marianno clan as just another bunch of thugs that needed to be dealt with. Harassment and threats were a normal part of his business. Bobbi would not take any chances. Dalca might be followed – she had to be careful. They would certainly be aware that he liked the ladies and that he might try to cash in on his leverage with Bobbi. She would be surprised if Marriano hadn't assumed as much.... She hadn't always thought like a criminal. She could thank Marko for that.

At first she didn't notice them.... The corridor was packed with people gathering for the arrival. It was a simple nod of the head that tipped her off. A young man in a sweatshirt tipped his hat across the walkway and glanced toward where Bobbi was waiting. Thirty feet directly in front of her, another man in a business suit returned the nod.

They returned their gazes toward the crowd gathering near the gate entrance. As flight #754 from San Jose pulled up to the hanger, both men stiffened. They again signaled each other in a subtle but certain manner. As others rose to greet the arrivals, the men sat. They watched the gate intently. The man closest to Bobbi signaled to another man who was standing by a row of lockers near the gate. They were waiting for someone. If it was Dalca, it could only be with the hopes that he would lead them to her. The flight was almost an hour late.

There was a restroom in the rear of the lounge. If Manuel came into the lounge looking for her, it would be her only recourse. She held her breath as Dalca stepped through the runway. He stopped and looked around. He left little doubt that he was expecting to be met by someone. He had only met her once, but he was sure he could recognize her. Two men fixed their eyes on him while the man closest to Manuel scanned the crowd for any sign of Bobbi. Manuel approached a woman that favored Bobbi but realized it wasn't her.

He stopped and looked toward the lounge where Bobbi was hiding and started walking toward it. As casually as she could, she quickly walked to the ladies room.

Dalca stood at the door of the lounge and looked around. She was nowhere to be found. *She surely wouldn't stand me up*, he thought. *I hold the purse strings to ten million dollars.* He stepped back onto the concourse and slowly headed toward the baggage area. The three men followed close behind.

Ten minutes later Bobbi emerged from the ladies room. She returned to her table and scanned the concourse. They were gone. She remained in the lounge for another drink and left one hour later.

Dalca stopped at the information desk and left word for Bobbi to call him at his hotel. She would not make the call.

Bobbi caught a cab and directed it back to her hotel. She withdrew $10,000 from the ATM in the hotel lobby before going to her room. She figured the bank could pinpoint the withdrawal point. She had no choice – she needed the money.

CHAPTER 21

"HELLO.... IS THIS GINA?" Rudy asked. Rudy called in case anyone but Gina answered the phone.

"Yes it is.... Who is this?" the Hanslow Plantation maid answered.

"Rudy Rogers, ma'am.... I'm a friend of Jake, I mean Salloa. He wanted me to call."

"Is he alright?"

"He's fine, thanks. I am a business associate of Salloa's... so to speak. We were wondering if you could meet us for coffee at the Beach Deli on 17 sometime soon?"

"I'd love to. I haven't seen Jake, I mean Salloa, in awhile. I miss that rascal."

"He is a loveable kind of guy," Rudy said.

"Loveable in a very strange way," Gina said. "I can meet you there in thirty minutes if that would work."

"Excellent.... We'll see you there," Rudy said giving Jake a nod and hanging up the phone. "Is she better looking than Jill?"

"Damn close," Jake said. They smiled and headed out the door.

* * * *

The Beach Deli crowd was slow Tuesday morning at 10:30. Except for a couple of local attorneys trying to make time with Jill, the place was quiet. Jake and Rudy took their customary window seat. Jill, seizing the opportunity to escape the long arm of the law, came to wait on the Strand Private Eye work force.

"Hey boys.... Care for anything hot?" She meant coffee of course.

"The hotter the better," Rudy chimed in.

"Ditto," Jake added.

She wiggled to the counter and came back with two cups of coffee for the dynamic duo.

"I would ask if you guys are up to any good, but I know better than that."

"We've been up to good way too long, my dear," Jake said. "Do you have anything in mind?"

"Sorry, Jake. You see those guys at the other end?"

Jake and Rudy nodded yes.

"Lawyers," she said. "You know how much I'm into cash."

"What we're packing money can't buy," Rudy said with his silly grin.

"Is that right?" she said with a wink as she meandered down to the legal department.

Gina Lacky slithered into the deli and scooted Jake a little closer to the window.

"Well hey, Salloa, or should I call you Jake?" she said with a gorgeous smile.

"What the heck, call me Jake. Just don't tell Marko."

"Deal," she said. "And you must be Rudy?" she said, extending her dainty hand toward him, which he promptly kissed. Jake felt a little nauseated.

"What's up?" she asked.

Jill came by with a coffee and set it in front of Gina who nodded her gratitude.

After Jill moved on, Jake said, "First of all, I'm not really a spiritual advisor for Mona."

Gina put her hand over her mouth in mock fashion and said, "No!"

"I know it's hard to believe. I would say I'm up for an Academy Award.... Anyway, Mona hired me to put a tail on Marko. Get video of his comings and goings at the townhouse, especially when it came to the women that he was bringing in and out. As you can imagine, he gave me plenty of material."

"So Mona is planning on cleaning his clock?"

"I guess so.... My curiosity was raised when those two thugs were at the plantation and beat the hell out of Marko. I thought, 'Why would Marko allow that in his own house?' I remembered what you said about possible mob involvement with some of their activities.... I did some checking, especially around the golf course."

"And?" she said after Jake hesitated in his discourse.

"And we came across something strange on the course. We sneaked onto the course the other night sometime after midnight and managed to get into a maintenance shack that had gotten our attention. Once inside we discovered that one of the walls had a considerable space behind it and no way to enter. We assumed that it was controlled by the computer system.... Do you have any idea what that could be about?"

Gina assumed a serious expression and cupped the coffee that Jill had just refilled. "I'm really not sure," she truthfully said. "Something is going on with Marko, but I don't know what it is.... I do know that something goes down the first Saturday of every month. It has ever since I've been there."

"Like what?" Rudy asked.

"Like some of the employees always work that day. It's always the same group. A select few are in on something every month. The dead couple were two of them.... If I had to guess

I would say something is dropped off Saturday morning and picked up Tuesday.... Always the first part of every month."

"What do you think it is?" Rudy asked.

"If I had to guess I would say drugs."

The three sat in silence and drank their coffee.

"And that Mason couple was part of it?" Rudy asked.

"Yes they were."

"What were they like?"

"Very sweet.... I never did believe that murder suicide crap," Gina said.

"Do you think their deaths had anything to do with the drugs or whatever is going on there?"

"I don't know. I wouldn't doubt it, but I don't know."

"It could play into your Mafia theory."

"If it's true and the Mafia is involved, it could be very bad for your health... especially if they think you are on to them," Gina said. "When the Mafia is involved, this girl is playing dumb – and you need to be careful," she said, sticking her finger into Jake's chest.

"As far as we're concerned, you don't know a thing about this. I give you my word," Jake said. "We are not going to put you in jeopardy."

"You were more silly as Salloa," Gina said with a wink.

"He's still pretty damn funny," Rudy said. "And his jokes aren't bad either."

"I can believe that," Gina said.

* * * *

Mona stood staring out the window on the back porch of the Hanslow Plantation. Marko sat in a chair behind her, gazing at the same view.

"Can you believe this?" Marko said.

205

"Believe it... like we have a choice?" Mona said. "Yeah, I would say this is a little too believable for my taste."

"Things should get back to normal soon," he said. "It's only a matter of time before they catch his ass. Holder better enjoy himself while he can. When Marianno gets a hold of him it won't be pretty."

"Larry Holder," she said with a laugh. Mona turned and looked directly at Marko. "If you weren't screwing his wife, none of this would have happened."

"Like you're perfect," Marko stewed. "Hell, you've screwed half the damn town."

"That's just like you to attack me when you're caught with your pants down. I ain't perfect, but I'm not the pig you've been and you damn well know it too!" Mona seethed.

Mona walked again to the window and said in a calmer voice "Your pal Theo called an hour ago.... They're still clueless. They can't get the bank in Costa Rica to give out any information. The account is dwindling daily. That's all they're saying."

"Does he think they're together?" Marko asked.

"He doesn't think so.... What do you think? You're the expert on the bitch."

"I doubt if they're together, but how the hell would I know?"

"Something else I've been thinking," Mona said. "What if he talks anyway? He's got the money.... What difference does it make to him? Either way, if he's caught, he's dead.... We're screwed if he talks. We'll have no rest until he's dead. That's for sure."

Twenty feet away in the hall Gina quietly slipped away, reeling from what she had just heard.

*   *   *   *

Jake noticed his answering machine light was blinking when he entered his house. He pressed play and had two messages. The first was from Sally. She wanted him to pick up beer on the way over. The other was from Mona Pasko. She told Jake that she would be suspending his services for the time being. The remaining money that she owed him would be sent in the mail. He should get it within the week. His golf privileges were also suspended.

Jake opened the backdoor and let in Amos. "Oh, well," he said to himself. He felt bad about getting paid so much by Mona to spy on Marko and then to turn around and uncover a potentially devastating crime scheme they had going on. His client could easily end up in jail.

He certainly had gathered the goods on Marko. If Mona wanted evidence, she had it. He left her the videotapes the last time he saw her.

The phone rang and he picked it up.

"Jake... this is Gina. Something has come up that I felt you needed to know. I found out a few minutes ago that Marko and Mona have been blackmailed by one of their employees at the Grounds Barn. A guy named Larry Holder. I've met him a time or two. He doesn't seem the blackmailing type, but oh well. I've been fooled before... Salloa."

"So what's the blackmail about?"

"I don't know. I overheard Marko and Mona talking. They didn't know I was around. She alluded to the fact that Marko was having an affair with the guy's wife. Her name is Bobbi."

"What does she look like?"

"Tall, long shapely legs, brunette, early thirties, short hair, good looking."

"I remember her. Marko saw her a number of times. So she was one of the workers, too?"

"That's right; she's one of the workers that do the deal each month…. She's Holder's wife. She has since split and no one knows where she is."

"She's not with Larry?" Jake asked.

"Doesn't look like it. From what I gathered, she knows that her husband has stuck Marko and she's on the run. At least that's what it sounds like to me."

"So Holder has the goods on Marko. It must be the deal going down at the Barn. Either pay up or he's gonna talk."

"That's the way I figure it, Jake," Gina said. "I'm sure that's why those thugs showed up and beat the shit out of Marko. His playing around put the whole operation in jeopardy."

"Wow…you've got to be right…. Do you think Bobbi's in on it?"

"I doubt it. I think it was Larry's doing…. I could be wrong…. This is getting too crazy, Jake. I'm gonna split. I'm telling Mona tomorrow that I'm out of here…. I'll tell her I have to go home. She knows I miss my mother, anyway. I'll talk to Herndon before I go. He needs to know what's going down…. Anyway, Jake, I just wanted to tell you what I found out. You need to be careful. These guys are not to be played with."

"I'll be careful. There's a limit to what this boy is willing to do. We're figuring that if we can get the right information, we can turn it over to the boys in the department."

"Well, anyway. You be careful, Jake. I'll always smile when I think of you."

"Thanks, Gina. Beware of spiritual advisors wearing robes," he said, smiling into the phone. "You take care, kid," he said, hanging up the receiver.

He called Rudy and relayed everything that Gina had told him.

CHAPTER 22

BOBBI LOOKED OUT THE WINDOW of her luxurious suite and contemplated her future. She had come to love life in Bogota but she had to flee. Now she was in one of the most exciting cities on earth and she was afraid to leave her hotel. Things had to get better than this.

Luckily she had checked in under another name other than her alias, Bobbi Thimpkin - Marko and Ellias both knew that one. Instead she went by Joan Smith. Otherwise, she would be on the run again. As it was she could sit it out right where she was.

From her fourth floor window, she had a view of the Ipanema Beach. Thousands of sunbathers wearing the skimpiest attire on earth covered the beach on this hot summer afternoon. She wished she could join them. *Maybe in a few days*, she thought.

Manuel Dalca would be pissed, no doubt. She figured to get up with him later. She was not against showing her gratitude. He would certainly understand.

It might be a while before he could see her. She might have to wait until his next trip to town. A man with cash certainly wouldn't have to do without companionship for long in Rio. It was hard to feel real sorry for him.

*   *   *   *

"Has anyone inquired about my whereabouts, a young lady perhaps?" Dalca asked the woman at the airport information desk.

"No sir," she said. "I have your number. We will direct any inquirers your way."

Manuel put down the phone. "Damn," he said. He had planned a four-day romp chasing Bobbi around his room. He would give her another day and then resort to plan "B" - which wasn't bad either. "What the hell, life is short," he said as he called room service for a massage and a margarita. A massage in Rio was definitely "full service."

*   *   *   *

"What you got?" Marianno asked from his Baltimore office.

"Nothing so far," the voice from the other end said. "He's holed up in his room. A gal showed up about an hour ago. She had a drink and a number of towels with her. She's still there, definitely not our girl. She's a shapely thing. He's not suffering I can tell you that."

"Nothing at the airport then?" Theo asked.

"Nothing.... He was expecting to be met at the airport. He did look around, scanned the crowd - looked in a couple of lounges. He was expecting someone that's for sure. He left a number he could be reached at on his way out. We have a man watching. No one has shown up. If he was looking for her, he got stood up."

"Yeah, the poor bastard," Theo said.

"You gotta feel for him. He's suffering as we speak," the voice said.

"Keep me informed. I'll call tomorrow. We'll confront the asshole then. He'll find out what not respecting Theo Marianno will get him," Theo said, hanging up. "Let's hope he enjoys the evening," he muttered to himself. "It'll be his last."

*   *   *   *

Jerry Uller, the former Larry Holder, drove his rental car the sixteen miles across treacherous roads to find the golf course he was looking for. He had heard the term "goat farm" used when describing golf courses in the states that left a little to be desired. At this course, that would be an accurate description. In fact, he thought he was looking at a pasture - a goat pasture at that, until he happened to see a loan golfer swatting away amongst the animals. The "Quito Golf" sign clued him in that he was at the right place.

"Bual Bleeaine?" Larry said, looking first at a piece of paper, then at the old, glassy eyed, unshaven man sitting on a keg-like barrel near a shack of a clubhouse. He hoped against hope that this was not the man he was looking for, but his hopes were soon dashed when the man nodded. Larry extended his right hand and said, "Jerry Uller."

The toothless man grinned and drooled all over himself. His grin turned into a laugh. He started to extend his hand when he slowly started to fall from his perch on the keg and found himself sprawled face down in the dirt.... Things were not looking overly promising.

A shapely brunette appeared from the clubhouse and stepped over the old fool, saying something to him in Spanish. The old man rolled out of her way and crawled around the corner.

"I'm sorry... he hasn't been the same since he lost the race for governor.... Just kidding." she said. "I'm Bual Bleeaine. You must be Jerry Uller."

There is a God, Larry thought. "Yes, I am," he said, extending his hand again.

"Did you have a good flight?" she asked.

"Yes, thank you."

"Please excuse Pedro. As you can see, he's not all there. He's supposed to be our starter. He can't even start himself.... Please come in," she said, motioning him to follow.

"Care for coffee?" she asked. He did and she poured them both a cup. They took a seat across from each other on a breezy, well-shaded patio.

"As you can see, the place could use some repair - not to mention some customers."

"I did notice a golfer down the hill a bit," Larry said.

"Lucky you. I think there are three customers on the course as we speak." She lit up a cigarette and took a long drag. She was about thirty with very pretty features. "I'm telling you these things so you will be sure you know what you are dealing with. This is not Augusta National."

"The setting's beautiful," Jerry said. "It looks to have potential. Do many people play golf in Quito?"

"There are a core group of golfers in Quito. Unfortunately, most of them play at the city course. It has a more convenient location and not as many animals on the course. People are more into tennis around these parts."

"I noticed the goats back there," he said, pointing back over his shoulder. "Are they wild?"

"No, they belong to the neighboring people. These are common people around here. They don't believe in fences and even if they did, they couldn't afford them."

"I see.... I must confess I was not expecting a woman, let alone a beautiful woman like yourself."

"Does that bother you, Mr. Uller?"

"Not at all."

"Good, my husband shares your sentiment. Let's grab a cart and I'll show you the spread."

"Sounds good," Jerry said.

They spent the next couple of hours touring the course and generally enjoying each other's company. They parted with the plan to meet again in a few days. The course was rough but had considerable potential.

*　　*　　*　　*

"This can't possibly work," Jake said with a puzzled look on his face.

Rudy looked at Jake and shook his head. "How you got along before I was hired will forever be a mystery to me.... I can't believe people paid you!"

They sneaked their way back into the Grounds Barn and were in the process of installing a motion detection video camera/transmitter. It was no bigger than a pack of cigarettes and could be activated by a timer or by a radio signal from anywhere within two miles of the Barn. The system came complete with a remote monitor so a live broadcast could be seen up to five miles away.

"Tell me again, who let you use this thing at the department?" Jake asked.

"It ain't none of your business, Jake." He fiddled with some more wires and stepped back to admire his handiwork. The camera was hidden in a crevice that would be just about impossible to notice. Someone would have to be paying very close attention to find it.

"Let's give it a test," Rudy said, holding up the radio transmitter. Jake was viewing the remote monitor across the room.

"I'm getting something!" Jake exclaimed.

"Keep it down, idiot. There might be somebody around!"

"Sorry, it's coming in clear. Now the camera is moving around. This is great."

"Great. We'll check it from the course Saturday. What time is our tee time?"

"8:15."

"Sounds good, let's go," Rudy said as he turned out the lights and left. He was digging this private eye stuff – not that he would admit it to Jake.

*　*　*　*

"Room service," the male voice said.

"Room service?" Manuel Dalca muttered as he went to the door and opened it. He was met with a forty-five mm sticking in his face.

"Surprise," one of the two intruders said to Dalca as they backed him into the room. "Have a good time last night? The girl looked hot!" Dalca did not speak. "Cat got your tongue, Mr. Dalca?"

"What's this about?" he finally managed.

"It's about respect."

"Respect?"

"Yeah, respect. You seem to be lacking in that area."

"What are you talking about?"

"Does the name Marianno ring a bell?"

"No, I...."

"How about Larry and Bobbi Holder... those names sound familiar?"

"Well... yes," Dalca said. "They're clients of the bank. They are Americans."

"It was expressed to you that their account was to be frozen. It hasn't been. That doesn't show respect."

"The bank policies are not mine. I have no control over them," he said, which was true enough.

"Have you heard from either of them?"

Manuel swallowed hard and said, "No."

"I don't believe you, and guess what, Mr. Marianno doesn't believe you either. You want the girl, don't you, Dalca? In fact you arranged for her to get out of Columbia. She was to come here to meet you. Isn't that right?" The barrel of the gun was resting on Dalca's temple at this point.

"Yes, yes. I was to meet her but she didn't show!" he said.

"You were looking for her when you got off the plane?"

"Yes, that's right. Please don't kill me... please!"

"You're having a bad week – first your hot rendezvous didn't show, and now this," the thug said with a smirk as he pulled the trigger. Dalca dropped like a bag of rice.

The silencer on the gun muffled the shot. They were out of the building in two minutes.

＊　　＊　　＊　　＊

Ralph Causey, the proprietor of the Third Avenue Pier, nodded as Jake trotted up to the counter with pole in hand.

Jake plopped down his three bucks and went out to try his luck. He didn't need any bait. He was gonna "spoon" it today. *"Probably nothing hitting anyway,"* Jake reasoned. Joe Lane, whom Jake had called to meet him, hadn't shown yet.

Two people were on the pier this early February morning. Jake didn't recognize either one of them. He flipped his spinner lure up and down the pier for forty minutes without any luck. Taking a break, he took a seat on a bench and popped the cola tab from his small cooler. A mild breeze blew in his face. Several minutes later he was aroused from his snooze by his obnoxious buddy, Joe.

215

"If you think I'm gonna listen to your ass snoring all afternoon, you better think again," Joe belted as he sat his stuff down next to Jake. "Where the hell is your bait?"

"Didn't get any," Jake said. "Thought I'd plug for some blues."

Joe shook his head. "If you had to live off what you catch, you would have been dead a long time ago."

"About time you got here," Jake muttered.

"Got caught up in traffic," Joe said.

That was a lie, Jake thought. The old fool could walk there in ten minutes. "Well, nothing's hitting."

"Really.... Have you put your pole in the water yet?"

"I've been up and down this pier, cowboy. Ain't nothing biting. And oh, by the way, nice pole," he said, referring to the new pole Joe was sporting. At their last encounter Joe had lost his pole over the rail.

"Kiss my ass," Joe said gazing across the ocean.

Jake and Joe spent the afternoon trading insults and tall tales. Neither had a bite. Joe made his usual wise cracks about Jake's private eye business and Jake continually reminded Joe how pitiful he was. It was just the kind of give-and-take they were used to. Jake needed a break and old Joe could always provide it.

CHAPTER 23

BOBBI'S FOURTH DAY IN RIO was another beautiful day in the big city. She figured with ten million people in the city, she should be able to scoot down to the beach and catch a few rays. That's exactly what she did.

Her string bikini was the "uniform of the day." After toasting each side and politely saying "no" to a couple of Brazilian bucks, she picked up her things and left.

She stopped for a sandwich at an open-air deli halfway back to her hotel. She picked up an English language daily paper and settled into a shady booth.

With her sandwich half eaten, she saw the small article on the third page. "Costa Rican business man found murdered." The breath went from her lungs as she read on, "Manuel Dalca, a Costa Rican banking executive, was found with a bullet wound to his head in his suite at the Airdale Plaza Hotel. The victim had been in the country two days and was last seen alive by a massage therapist who had visited him the night before. The victim was presumed murdered. The therapist was not a suspect."

A wave of nausea suddenly came over her. She cleared her table and made her way thirty feet down the street before she spilled her guts on the sidewalk. She raced to her room at a frantic pace, just short of running. She dashed into the lobby and nodded toward the desk clerk. She hopped an elevator and went to her room, dead-bolting the door behind her.

"Oh, my God!" she said as she lay gasping on her bed.

* * * *

"Haven't seen you boys lately. Where you been?" Bob Burly said to Jake and Rudy as they walked into the clubhouse at Droughbrigh Country Club Saturday morning at 7:30.

"Free golf's over. Kind of cramps my style. Know what I mean?" Jake said.

"It ain't that bad. You can still get a senior rate."

"It ain't bad, but it ain't free," Rudy chimed in.

"Yeah, yeah.... Anyway, boys, I got you down for 8:15. Get up with Birdie. He'll fix you up."

The boys wandered into the grill area and ordered a couple of biscuits from Ginger.

"Here you go, boys," she said in her usual sultry voice.

"Used to be a club dancer," Jake said to Rudy, but not loud enough for her to hear.

"I can believe that," Rudy replied.

The food and the view were excellent. They finished breakfast and got up with Birdie.

"You're free to go," Birdie said. "Those guys are waiting on somebody," he said, pointing to three men on the putting green.

That sounded good to Jake and Rudy. They smacked their drives two hundred yards down the fairway - needless to say, they were pleased.

No one was ahead of them so they hustled along to get some space between themselves and the foursome coming up behind them. They did not foresee any problem. They were looking for a truck of some type to pull along the seventh fairway right about 9:00 A.M. They arrived in location with ten minutes to spare.

Just like clockwork, a large panel truck pulled down the road going right past them. The side of the truck said "Porter Transport." Rudy switched the remote control camera on and within a few seconds the picture came up. Rudy scanned the lens around the building.

The rollup door was open. A man was sitting at the computer station and a woman stood in the middle of the open door. A moment later another man appeared. Jake and Rudy recognized him as the man who caught them snooping around the building a couple of weeks before. A moment later the truck came into view backing into the building. A lone driver stepped out.

"Hey, good looking," John Browner said to Marie as he stepped out of his truck.

"Hey," Marie said, not giving him any encouragement. "Where's your paperwork?"

"Easy, darling," he said. "Here you go."

"John," her husband, Sam, said. "Good trip?"

"Great."

The voices sounded muffled to Jake and Rudy but the picture was crystal clear.

Ted Miller drove a forklift up onto the truck. Sam punched some keys on the computer and the wall in the back began to lift, revealing a sizeable storage area that was completely empty.

The first four pallets appeared to be normal golf course supplies: fertilizer, grass seed, lime, etc. The rest of the load was a different story. The remaining eight pallets were filled with large bags of what seemed to be more of the same, maybe twelve on a pallet. They were neatly stacked in the secret area. Once the truck was empty the secret door went down and the truck pulled out. The maintenance overhead door closed when the truck left.

Jake and Rudy watched the proceedings carefully. "You in the mood for Tuesday morning golf?" Jake asked Rudy.

"Wouldn't miss it for the world."

They sped off in their cart as the trailing foursome approached.

*   *   *   *

Larry Holder signed the papers as Jerry Uller and became the new owner of Quito Golf. The purchase price was two million dollars. He was happy with the deal. Bual Bleeaine and her husband were even happier. As a new landowner, Ecuadorian law provided Jerry the opportunity to become a full citizen. He did just that.

His first order of business was to change the name from Quito Golf to "Quito Golf, Racket Club and Resort." With his own computer knowledge and with the help of a local geek, he would construct a Web page that would inform the world of this new great attraction. The Racket Club part would help bring in local business.

Contractors would be brought in to: rebuild the clubhouse, repave the tennis courts, put a fence around the property, build a twenty-unit deluxe mountain-top motel, and rework the greens and sand traps. The estimated cost would take another four million. The funds to cover it had already been switched to a local account.

The original Costa Rican account was now three million and change. If not for the possibility that Bobbi might need the money, he would have pulled it all out. Not a night went by that he didn't wonder where she was. He prayed that she was alright.

Sand Trap

*   *   *   *

Bobbi's daily routine consisted of a careful walk to the neighborhood deli. There she would order a sandwich and drink. Every day she bought an English-language paper and bottled water. She wore sunglasses and a ball cap pulled low across her forehead along with loose-fitting, full-length jeans.

She was a beautiful, wealthy young woman, in one of the most exciting cities on earth, and she felt like a prisoner. She thought about fleeing the country, but where could she go? She had to assume the Mafia had ordered Dalca's death and had followed him to Rio hoping he would lead them to her. How much he had talked before they blew his brains out she didn't know. They had to be watching the airports, docks, train, and bus stations. They were certainly still in town. By now they probably had enlisted their South American brothers in crime to assist in the hunt. There were one-hundred-and-fifty hotels in Rio. Eventually they would all be checked. Her friendly hotel clerk could probably be bought if anyone made an offer. She felt trapped.

Six months earlier she had been an unhappy wife, trapped in an illegal occupation. She had spent her entire adult life looking over her shoulder.

It amazed her how often she thought about Larry. She had convinced herself that getting him out of her life was the best thing she could do. Now despite flings with two of the most exciting men she had ever known, she found herself thinking of Larry almost exclusively.

She had always blamed the state of their marriage on him. Looking back on it now, she realized that she was as much at fault as he was. Not that any of that made much difference now - for all she knew he was dead. She certainly would not see him again.

She drank her bottled water while sitting on her balcony. Despite everything else on the horizon, the statue of Jesus always caught her eye. Religion had seemed like such a waste of time to her - a pastime for weak people. She found herself staring at the statue more and more. Not normally an emotional person, lately she found herself openly weeping. Was it her desperate situation or rather her recognition of spiritual bankruptcy? She wasn't sure. The statue was the last sight she saw each evening and the first sight she saw every morning. Somehow that hunk of marble gave her a sense of comfort. She couldn't explain it. Something was changing in her psyche.

CHAPTER 24

I T WAS A CRISP MONDAY MORNING at the Grounds Barn and the crew was cranking up.

"What's that?" Marie Conner asked, pointing toward an object tucked between the beams on the side-wall.

"What's what?" Sam asked.

"Right up there.... That little white thing with a black dot on it."

"Oh, yeah... I see it," Sam said. He pulled up the twelve-foot extension ladder and climbed up for a closer look. "It's a camera.... Somebody put a camera up here," he said looking down at his wife with a "can you believe it" look.

"Who would do that?" Marie asked.

"I don't know," Sam said still standing on the top of the ladder. "Marko wouldn't do it. I mean... why would he?"

"Why would he spy on us? We've never given him any reason to," Marie said. "Maybe Bobbi and Larry cutting out has made him nervous."

"I can't believe he'd do it, I mean... why?"

"What's going on?" Ted asked as he stepped into the barn.

"We found a camera," Marie said, pointing up to where her husband was.

"A camera?"

"A camera," Sam said. "My guess it's a remote-control variety. It's positioned for a perfect view of the false door." That statement raised some eyebrows.

"Damn," Ted said. "Whoever planted it would have a perfect view of the delivery and pickup. I wonder how long it's been there?"

"I don't think it's been there too long. I notice stuff like that," Marie said. "How could anyone get in here? I thought this place was too secure to be broken into."

"Evidently not." Ted said.

"It's probably controlled from a remote location... not more than a mile or so away. Maybe somewhere on the golf course," Sam said. "I haven't noticed anybody suspicious around here."

They stood there in silence thinking.

"Wait a minute," Ted said. "There were two clowns sneaking around here a couple of weeks ago. One of them was trying to get in the building. When I confronted them they said they were looking for their ball."

"In the building?" Marie asked.

"That's what I asked them. They seemed like a couple of goofballs so I shooed them off. I didn't think any more of it."

"Somebody is on to us. There's no other reason for a camera.... I wonder who was playing golf Saturday morning with a tee time between eight and nine?" Ted asked.

They looked at each other and made their way to the clubhouse. Bob Burly gave them the names of the golfers who played Saturday morning between eight and nine.

Ted gave Bob and Birdie Malone the description of the snooping golfers. They compared the description with the sign-in log and they had a match - Jake Brown and his golfing buddy Rudy.

*   *   *   *

Marie Conner opened her email and was about to delete the mass of jokes and foolishness when one message caught her eye. It was from a hotmail address from a sender named "bigbrowneyes." That was the nickname that Marie had given Bobbi. She clicked on the email. It read:

Dear Marie,

I have missed you guys so much. I can't tell you where I am because it would be too dangerous. Enough to say that I am out of the country. Marianno's thugs have somehow found the city I'm in. I'm afraid to leave my hotel room. They have already killed a male friend of mine who they thought would lead them to me. I'm scared to death!

Do you have an email address or anyway I could get in touch with Larry? I don't know if he's dead or alive. I pray that he's alive. If he isn't please tell me. I have no one to turn to now and Larry is the only one I can think of. I wouldn't blame him if he didn't want to help me. I just don't know where else to turn.

I've been on the run for weeks. Tell Sam and Ted that I miss them very much. Don't try to track me down. Believe me, it's way too dangerous.

I love you, Bobbi

She returned the email with the following note:

Dear Bobbi,

I'm so glad that you're alive. We're all so worried, not only about you but also about Larry. Things are crazy here. We discovered a remote-control video camera in the barn today. It looks like someone has seen us do the drop and maybe more. We have an idea who it might be. We're going to call him later this evening to find out what it's all about. We could be looking at jail time. We're all scared.... Everything is going to hell.

We haven't heard anything from Larry. All I know is that Marko's pissed. I've got an old hotmail address for Larry. I don't know if it's active or not. It's larry2245817@jero.com. Like I say, I have no idea if it's still valid or not. We've tried to reach him at it but we've never got an answer back. On the positive side it hasn't been returned as a bad address so I don't know.

I'm not much for praying but I've prayed for you and Larry every day for months. We miss you both! Please keep in touch!

Love, Marie

*   *   *   *

"Is this Jake Brown?"

"Yes it is," Jake said, picking up the phone. Sally McSwain was resting her head on his lap and watching TV.

"Mr. Brown... my name is Ted Miller. I talked to you and your friend briefly the other day at Droughbrigh Country Club. You were looking for your ball near one of the maintenance barns. I'm afraid I was a little short with you and I asked you to move on."

Jake straightened in his chair. Sally sat up, sensing it was a rather important call. "Yes.... I remember," Jake said, pushing the record button.

"I work with two others at the barn, a husband and wife, Sam and Marie Conner. We would like to meet with you somewhere for a chat, hopefully sometime Wednesday. We would like to speak with your friend also. Would that be possible?" They knew that Jake and Rudy had a Tuesday morning tee time.

"How did you know who I was?"

"I did a little investigating. Could we meet Wednesday?"

They must have found the camera, Jake thought. *Why else would I be getting a call?* "Wednesday would be good," Jake said. "I don't see a problem.... What's this about?"

"I'm not at liberty to say right now. We'll talk Wednesday. Is there a place you'd like to meet, maybe in the morning?"

"How about the Beach Deli on King's Highway?"

"The Beach Deli sounds good."

"You know where it is?"

"Absolutely. We can meet you there at nine," Ted said.

"I'll see you there at nine. We'll be waiting for you."

Jake hung up the phone and exhaled deeply.

Jake always did that when he was stressed. "Must be serious," Sally said.

"Serious, I don't know.... Interesting, definitely."

He dialed Rudy's number and gave him the news.

*   *   *   *

Bobbi pulled out the laptop that she had bought several days earlier and composed this email to Larry:

Dear Larry,

I don't know where to begin except to say that I'm sorry. Something had to give with us. I saw my way out and I took it. Looking back, I am not proud of myself, but I did what I did.

I got to hand it to you. It took some kind of balls to do what you did. It's too bad we couldn't have pulled it off together. I blew the hell out of that plan. I hope you're still alive. I've found myself thinking of you a lot lately. I guess that's all water under the bridge now.

Marko and Marianno are after me, too. I've been on the run for weeks. I have accessed some of the money, not a lot, $10,000. I'm in Rio de Janeiro. Manuel Dalca arranged for my escape from Columbia. Marko had me set up there in an apartment.... I'm sorry. Anyway, Dalca was to meet me here. He was expecting a payback because he arranged for me to get out of Columbia. There's a lot going on in my life that I'm not proud of.

I saw Marianno's thugs waiting for him at the airport when he arrived. They didn't see me. Dalca looked for me but I hid from him when I saw that he was being watched. Bottom line is, they murdered him three days later. They killed him in his hotel room.... Shot him in the head execution style. I'm sure they're still here. They have to figure that I'm in the city somewhere.

I'm afraid to leave my room. I'm in room 406 at the Imperial Hotel... Is there anyway you could help me escape? I wouldn't blame you if you told me to go to hell. I'm scared and I don't know where to turn. If you get this please email me.

Love, Bobbi

She pressed "send" as a tear rolled down her cheek. She turned toward the statue in the distance and cried.

CHAPTER 25

JAKE AND RUDY VIEWED the Malpass Trucking pickup. It was right on time Tuesday morning. Ted, Sam, and Marie pretended not to notice the camera that was following their actions. When the truck left, Ted went to the clubhouse to confirm what they already knew - Jake Brown and Rudy Rogers were on the golf course.

*　　*　　*　　*

Jake and Rudy arrived at the Beach Deli 8:45 Wednesday morning. They took a large window booth and waited for their guests.

"You have enough room?" Jill Arthur asked them as she set down two cups of coffee.

"Sometimes a person just needs a little elbow room," Jake chirped in.

"We were hoping for a table dance." Rudy quipped, the dirty old man coming out of him.

"Don't count on it, old man," Jill said. "You need to teach him some manners," she said turning to Jake. She was not pleased.

"I've tried... believe me I've tried," Jake said. Even he was embarrassed by Rudy's occasional crassness.

She took their order and left in a huff.

"I'm sorry, already," Rudy said to Jake. "What do you think they'll want?"

"We'll find out in a few."

Two minutes after nine, Ted Miller and the Conners entered the Beach Deli and joined Jake and Rudy.

After introductions and placing their order, Jake asked, "So what's the deal?"

After hesitating a moment Sam said, "We found something suspicious at our place of employment. We thought maybe you might know something about it."

Jake and Rudy gave each other a "what is he talking about?" look and Jake said, "Go on."

"Someone placed a remote control camera on a rafter in the Barn. It was well hidden. It's a wonder we saw it. We're sure it was placed there to spy on us."

"Why would anyone want to watch you work?" Rudy asked.

"Good question," Sam continued. "I guess some people are just a little too nosey."

"So what's the problem?" Jake said. "Unless of course you had something to hide. You're not hiding anything are you?"

"Why don't we just knock off the B.S.," Ted said. "I saw you assholes snooping around the building playing stupid, which, incidentally, you do well. Bottom line is, we think you planted the camera. You spied on us Saturday morning and Tuesday morning from the golf course. We think you know exactly what's happening there. Tell me I'm wrong."

Rudy sipped the last of his coffee and leaned back against the window examining the golf course crew. "Quite an operation you've got there, kids," he said. "First class all the way, no doubt.... Problem is, it could get you ten years."

The three visitors stiffened as Rudy talked.

"I like the wall - computer operated, quite impressive. I imagine they pay flunkies like you quite well to do the dirty work - a nice setup... especially if you can get some pawns to take the fall for you. The big boys don't like to get their hands dirty. Why should they? That's your job." Rudy was working them for a reaction and he was going to get one.

"We ain't taking the fall alone. I can tell you that. The whole house is coming down if they take me down," Marie said.

"You could always try blackmail, it's been done before. You might even live to enjoy it," Jake said.

"Who told you about them?" Sam asked.

"Who you talking about?" Jake said, playing dumb.

"Bobbi and Larry Holder. You know damn well who we're talking about."

"Let's see now, we have the Holders, hiding somewhere with a bag of money, and then there's you guys, scared to death and trapped," Jake said.

"Are you guys cops?" Marie asked.

"I'm not a cop - private eye. Mona hired me to keep an eye on Marko. One thing led to another and here we are. Rudy's a retired cop. We don't have an agenda, just taking one step at a time - which led us to you."

"We're not criminals. We never expected this shit. Larry and Bobbi didn't expect this. We were stupid kids, just Navy punks who got caught up in this mess. We had no idea," Sam said as the other two nodded in agreement.

"Look, I don't think you're hard core criminals, ok? And I don't believe that you ever intended for this to go this far. But here you are and the law is the law."

"Are you going to turn us in?" Marie said, starting to tear up.

"Just calm down," Rudy said. "I think if you cooperate, the judge might cut you some slack. I know for a fact the vice squad is after the big boys. They're not that concerned with the little fish in the pond. If you play along you might not do time. I can't promise anything, but I've seen how these things work."

They sat in silence and Sam finally spoke, "What do you want from us?"

"Information," Rudy said. "Like Jake said, I'm retired from the Myrtle Beach PD. I'll set up a meeting time at the station and we'll all get together and talk."

"Will we go to jail?" Marie asked still fighting back the tears.

"I doubt it you will. That decision will be made later. Are you willing to talk?" Rudy asked. Rudy could see that they were shaken, especially the girl. "Listen... I think if you guys cooperate, things could go easy for you.... Question is, are you willing to talk?"

"We're willing," Ted said with the backing of the others.

*   *   *   *

Bobbi munched on her sandwich with one eye on the paper and the other scanning the crowd. Paranoia was her natural state these days.

At first she didn't see him. It might have been his peeking over his sunglasses that tipped her off. A bearded man in his late twenties stood at a corner across the street and was peering over the top of his newspaper and scanning the crowd. He seemed especially interested in women with Bobbi's age and build - not in the usual flirtatious way so prevalent in Latin America. He was looking for someone in particular.

She peeked over her paper and watched. Suddenly, he fixed his eyes on her, focusing intensely. His gaze never drifted from her. As calmly as she could she finished her meal, being careful not to let on that she knew she was being watched. She plotted her next move - would he continue to watch or would he approach her? If he tried to follow her, and he certainly would if she started to leave, she had to lose him before she got back to the hotel. As terrifying as that very real possibility was, it was not near as bad as waiting for him to show up at her table. She had to try to lose him.

From where she was sitting the quickest way out of his sight was in a direction opposite of the hotel. The closest corner was twenty seconds away. From where he was, it would take him thirty seconds to get there even if he ran. She would try to lose him at the corner. She had no idea what lay around the corner. She would just have to take her chances.

She rose slowly, stretched, and picked up her purse. She grabbed her stuff and casually walked to the trashcan, depositing her wrapper. Out of the corner of her eye she saw him put the paper down. Taking a quick breath, she strolled quickly toward the corner.... He began his pursuit.

When she got to the corner her heart sank. It was nothing but a side alley between two city blocks. There were no cars or people, just a walk ten feet wide and two hundred feet long. She strode forward. Halfway through, she heard the steps behind her - her heart quickened. Should she run or just keep walking? She kept walking. A run would be a dead give away. If she walked he would keep his distance. Despite her brisk pace she could tell he was gaining on her. Forty more feet to the other side and he was eighty feet behind her and closing.

Arriving at the next intersection, she had to think quickly. It was a busy city street. Panic has set in full bore on Bobbi. Her pursuer was less than sixty feet behind her. Traffic sped by as she made her move - jumping in front of a speeding cab. The driver slammed on his brakes barely missing her. She ran around and jumped in the side and screamed for him to go. The driver, evidently used to this kind of thing, sped off as she gasped the name of her hotel. She didn't have to tell him to hurry. He could see the terror in her voice and eyes. Her pursuer, originally within an arm's length of the cab, was frantically trying to keep up by foot. The lights were green as the cab raced ahead, creating space between her and her pursuer.

The hotel came into view and she pulled out much more money than the driver needed from her purse. She showed it to him, stuck it in his shirt pocket and pointed to the front door. Her body language said "haul ass." She did not need an interpreter. He nodded his head and pulled to the front door of the hotel - coming to a screeching stop. She quickly got out.

A hotel patron approached the cab for a ride. The driver sped off in the opposite direction from which they had just come, leaving the patron spewing profanities. Bobbi was already in the lobby.

Out of breath and arriving at the elevator, she rode it to the fourth floor. Looking out the large window next to the elevator she watched the front of the hotel. Not ten seconds later she saw the man who had been following her hurrying along the sidewalk in front of the hotel. He stopped for a moment and looked at the hotel. He appeared to make a mental note and kept on going. Bobbi went to her room and vomited her lunch. She could not stop shaking.

Chapter 26

H IS HEART WAS IN HIS THROAT when he saw the email from "bigbrowneyes." He opened the email reading it four times. His response was simply, "Hold fast... I'm on my way, Larry." He made arrangements for the next flight to Rio. He would be there in twenty hours.

*   *   *   *

"Have a seat," Detective Jeremy Edwards said. Officer Edwards had been the top Myrtle Beach officer in drug enforcement for several years.

Sam and Marie Conner, Ted Miller, Rudy Rogers, and Jake Brown made their way into one of the PD meeting rooms and took a seat around the large table. All eyes were fixed on Mr. Edwards.

"Sergeant Rogers has informed me concerning the rough details regarding this case. He stated that though you are technically guilty, in a certain sense you have been victims of circumstances. I want you to speak freely. There are strong elements involved in this case: drugs, money, influential people, Mafia involvement. I am sure you're apprehensive and you need to know that we understand and appreciate your concerns. I want to assure you that your safety will be a primary concern of the Myrtle Beach Police Department.

"If what you can tell us is substantial enough to bring charges against the major players in question, the Witness Protection Program would certainly be in order.... Are you familiar with the Witness Protection Program?"

"New names, new locations, that kind of thing?" Sam asked.

"That's right," Detective Edwards said. "It's really more prevalent than you would think. Do you have any questions?"

They sat in silence. The Witness Protection Program sounded good. A fresh start in life was more than they had expected. They were thinking possible jail time - instead they may be getting a new lease on life.

Edwards looked over his glasses and asked, "When did you meet Marko and Mona Pasko?"

Ted Miller fielded the question. "We met them in a bar in Charleston nine years ago. They invited us to a party at his brother's house in Charleston."

"And his brother's name is?"

"Harone... Harone Pasko," Ted said.

"Does he still live in Charleston?"

"Yes."

"Is he involved with the drugs?"

"Yes. He owns Porter Transport. They bring the stuff to us."

Ted, Sam and Marie went on to tell everything they knew about the Pasko and Marianno involvement, including the ordeal with Larry and Bobbi Holder. They talked about the deaths of Hannah and Mike Mason and their suspicions of foul play. They spoke for several hours and were told not to leave the area. They were to carry on their jobs just like nothing had happened. When the time was right, the police department would dictate their next step. They needed to be packed up and ready to move. One phone call from the police and they were to leave in a moment's notice, no questions asked. They left the Myrtle Beach Police Department a lot more hopeful than when they arrived.

*   *   *   *

Jeremy Edwards made the necessary arrangements for the Witness Protection Program for the three workers. The plan was to get a search warrant served to Marko and Mona Pasko, Harone Pasko, and Theo Marianno, summoning them to Myrtle Beach to meet with the authorities. A search warrant would also be issued to search the Grounds Barn.

On the day of the search, Ted, Sam, and Marie would leave the area and begin their new lives in another location. They would remain in the new location and only return long enough for the trial. They requested to stay together so arrangements were made for them to relocate to Cleveland, Tennessee. They would be set up with decent jobs and paid for homes, compliments of the federal government.

*   *   *   *

Bobbi was limiting her food to what she could get from the vending machine on her floor. She was living on chips, candy bars, and soft drinks. She routinely checked the view from the window overlooking the street, looking for anything suspicious.

She saw him walk toward the hotel. It was the same man who had followed her two days before. Before entering, he met two other men on the sidewalk in front of the hotel, one older and one his age. They looked around glancing toward the front door. She watched as two men disappeared into the hotel and the other walked across the street and leaned against a light pole standing patrol. From his location, he could watch anyone who would come or go from the front door. Terrified, Bobbi ran back into her room.

She had seen the email note from Larry the night before. She prayed that he would not be walking into a trap.

*   *   *   *

Larry touched down in Rio on schedule and took a cab from the airport to the Imperial Hotel. He had the driver stop two blocks away. The driver pointed him toward the hotel and he proceeded with caution on foot. The fast pace of Rio de Janeiro stood in stark contrast to the "nobody's in a hurry" attitude of Quito.

He rounded the corner and the Imperial Hotel came into view. The front of the hotel had very little foot traffic. From the tone of her letter, he decided it might be dangerous to go straight to her room. His plan was to get a room directly beneath hers or as near to that as possible. She was in 406, he would ask for 306.

As he entered the lobby he noticed two men vigorously talking to a clerk at one end of the counter. He went to a female clerk at the other end of the counter - room 306 was available. He overheard one of the men at the counter say "She's tall, brunette, nice legs.... I know she's staying here. We've seen her come in."

The interrogators were insistent and intimidating. The clerk was trying to tell them that the hotel did not divulge information concerning their guests. It was obvious from the way the clerk was answering that Bobbi was in the hotel. The men were relentless, like wolves in a feeding frenzy. Larry turned away so they could only see his back.

Fortunately, the route to the elevators was away from the men. Larry got on the elevator and went to his room. He would have to act quickly. They could be on the way to her room at any time. They were not going to take "no" for an answer from the downstairs clerk.

In the room Larry went to the patio and climbed up on the top of the patio rail. The concrete pool was seventy feet below. He took an umbrella and began to smack it on Bobbi's patio rails.

She was on her bed staring at the ceiling. Terror, tension, and confusion dominated her mind. For one of the few times in her life, she found herself praying for help.

When she first heard the sound she thought it might have been the air conditioning. But no... that wasn't it. It was coming from the patio area. She went to the door and saw the tip of the umbrella beating against the rail, *What the hell?* she thought. She cautiously opened the sliding door.

Larry heard the door open and called out, "Bobbi, it's me, Larry!"

She gasped and ran to the rail and looked down. Their eyes met in a way that said more than words could convey. It was the most welcome sight that either one had ever seen.

"Larry!" she choked through tears.

"They're in the lobby. We have to move quickly! They'll be at your room any minute. They're giving the clerk hell downstairs. The clerk was getting flustered. He'll cave in."

"Oh, God... someone's at my door!" she cried.

"I'm holding on to the ledge. I've got a good grip. Lower yourself down the rails slowly as far as you can go. I'll grab you and pull you in."

"I can't! You know I hate heights!"

"You've got to do it! Close the patio door behind you. Do it now! I won't let you fall!"

"I can't!"

"Do it!" Larry ordered.

Bobbi looked at the statue in the distance and silently cried, "Dear God, please help me." She closed the patio door and threw one leg over the rail and began to lower herself down. She trembled as her feet left the security of the concrete floor and her body began to dangle eighty feet above the ground. She was fully extended before she felt Larry's hand on her knee. Her pursuers were pounding on her apartment door.

"Just a few more inches, baby. Come on, honey, you can do it."

"Oh, God," she said. "Please help me... Larry, help!"

He reached as far as he could but he could not get a good grip. "Swing back and forth a little. You have to come this way," he said.

"I can't!"

"Yes you can! You have to!"

She started to rock back and forth. Larry was able to get a better grip half way up her thigh.

"Hold it right there. When I tell you to let go, then let go." He got a grip with one arm around her upper thigh and the other holding on to a lip on the top ledge of his patio. When she let go he would have to allow her to drop into his arms and hope that he could stop her fall with the other hand. He looked at the statue in the distance and said, "Me and you, Lord.... Let go, Bobbi!"

She let go.... The sheer force of her fall jolted Larry to the point that he was sure he would lose his grip. Somehow he hung on. He steadied himself and gently turned her toward the patio floor. "Step off, honey," he said. She did and he joined her as they fell into each other's arms.

"Oh, Larry," Bobbi said through tears with her arms wrapped tightly around his neck.

"We got to get out of here.... I have a plan."

In his room was a large, heavy duty, roll-a-way suitcase. "Get in here. You're going out in this."

She could see it might work. She curled up inside and Larry zipped it shut. He pulled her out of the door and to the elevator.

One floor above, the men had forced their way into Bobbi's room. They found her belongings but no Bobbi. They looked the room over including the deck. She was nowhere to be found.

Meanwhile, down below in front of the hotel, Larry was hailing a cab.

"Petropolis.... Do you go to Petropolis?" Larry asked the driver. Petropolis was a sizeable town thirty miles away.

"Petropolis, no problem.... Let me help you with your bag," the driver said as he opened his trunk.

"No, that's all right. I want it in the seat with me."

"Whatever," the driver said as Larry lugged the bag in with all the strength he had. The driver sped off and they were gone.

CHAPTER 27

TED, SAM, AND MARIE GOT THE CALL on a
Wednesday evening. They were to be at the Myrtle
Beach Airport at 12:30 A.M. They would leave on a
late-night flight to Atlanta. There they would pick up a rental
car for the drive to Cleveland.... They didn't miss their flight.

The following morning Marko and Mona were rudely
awakened by the MB Police Department and served with a
search warrant for the Grounds Barn and were ordered to go
downtown. They were loaded into a squad car and driven to
police headquarters.

A troop of federal marshals called on Theo Marianno and
transported him to Myrtle Beach. At the same time the
Charleston Police Department, in conjunction with the Myrtle
Beach Department, escorted Harone Pasko north.

*   *   *   *

The cab driver came to a stop in the town-square in
Petropolis, Brazil. Larry paid him his fare and tugged the
suitcase from the cab. Tipping his hat to the driver, he pulled
the suitcase to a nearby park and found a table in the shade. He
unzipped the suitcase and she came tumbling out.

"You ok?" he asked. She was covered with sweat as she rolled from the baggage and stretched out on the lawn.

"Never better," she said, looking straight up at Larry with an ear to ear grin. "I'm so happy to see you.... I love you, Larry."

"I love you, too," he said through tears.

He knelt beside her and took her into his arms. She pulled away and looked him in the eyes and said, "I'm sorry for what I did. I wouldn't have blamed you for leaving me to die."

"I couldn't do that.... I'd rather die myself." She buried her head into his shoulder and wept.

After several minutes of embracing Larry said, "We need to contract a driver to Vitoria. It's a six-hour drive. From there we should be safe to catch a flight.... And oh, by the way, you're new name is Elizabeth Roberta Uller."

"Who?"

"I'll tell you on the way," he said with a wink as they walked off hand in hand.

*   *   *   *

"Let's go... were going to be late for church," Ray Coy said to his wife Debra.

"I'm ready," she said as she grabbed her purse and Ray pulled their front door open.

Elaine stood on the stoop with a tear trickling down her face. Daisy was in her mother's arms, holding a flower. Both were gazing at the front door.

*   *   *   *

The spring breeze felt good blowing across his face as Jake sat on the Third Avenue Pier and waited for the next bite.

Fishing had been pretty good. He'd already caught twenty keepers. It had been a month since the mess at Droughbrigh went down. The trial was being delayed until sometime next year. Marko, Mona, Marko's brother Harone, and Theo Marianno were all out on bail. It looked like they would all do time. If the murder charge concerning the Mason kids stuck, they could do more than time. Mona might escape prison.... That remained to be seen. For the time being, Droughbrigh Country Club was still open for business.

As far as Jake knew, Ted Miller and the Conners were resettled somewhere, and by all accounts, damn happy about it. No one knew what happened to Larry and Bobbi Holder. If they were still alive, they were several million dollars richer. Jake figured they were alive somewhere. The off-shore account had been depleted of funds – somebody had to do it.

Sally McSwain was still Jake's steady girl, even if he wasn't the best dancer in town. Rudy and Jake played golf almost every week... and yes... Jill Arthur still had the prettiest darn legs in Myrtle Beach!

Books by Dennis Gimmel
Dog Lot
Sand Trap
Conversations With Eunice

Order Form

To order additional copies, fill out this form and send it along with your check or money order to: Stellar Books, 706 Impala Ave., High Point NC 27265

Cost per copy $13.95 includes P&H.

Or order on line at:
  www.oldmp.com/sandtrap.htm

Ship _____ copies of *Sand Trap* to:

Name_____

Address:_____

City/State/Zip:_____

❏   Check box for signed copy